THE
PALE
INVADERS

THE
PALE
INVADERS

G. R. Kestavan

Atheneum

New York   1976

LIBRARY OF CONGRESS CATALOGING IN PUBLICATION DATA
Kesteven, G. R.   The pale invaders.

SUMMARY: The inhabitants of the secluded valley believe life has always been as they know it until strangers arrive who lend threatening reality to the tales of an elder about life before the devastating Upheaval.

[1. Science fiction] I. Title.
PZ7.C8823Pal5   [Fic]   75–25509
ISBN 0–689–30505–2

Copyright © 1974 by G. R. Crosher
All rights reserved
Manufactured in the United States of America by
Halliday Lithograph Company
West Hanover, Massachusetts
Designed by Nora Sheehan
First American Edition

Ke
11-12

Contents

THE
PALE
INVADERS

Old Carz

OLD CARZ, as we always called him, lived in the hut built against the Wall high up the valley. Ordinarily we children did not see much of him. Every few days Carole, who was the oldest girl, walked up with his supply of oatmeal and potatoes, and meat if we had enough, but otherwise, except when we carried down his store of fuel, we seldom had reason to go to the hut. And we were all a little afraid of him.

I realize now that his twisted foot, the result of an accident in his young days, might have become so painful as he aged as to deepen the lines on his leathery face and twist them into the fierce expression he so often wore; but then we saw only the thin line of a mouth, tightly held, and above his tangled beard the penetrating stare of his eyes from under their thick, jutting brows. We were not to reason that they might have arisen more from pain than from ill temper. And when he spoke, his voice had a harsh rasp to it that made us answer his questions briefly and get away as soon as we could.

His name was really Paul, but he was always known to us as "Old Carz." The nickname, prompted by our fear of him, arose from the tales of the Old Days that he had been known to tell. In the Old Days, so he would say, people had carz. And if any of us ventured to ask what a carz was, he would start on a strange story about people travelling around in a kind of iron box-on-wheels that went by itself, that was not pulled by anyone or even a horse or an ox. But we seldom gave him the chance to add more, for the absurdity of such a story would start us off laughing—usually led by eight-year-old John whose round face was always on the point of laughter. And we would run away down the valley calling out "Old Carz!" and John would pretend he was in a carz and run a swerving course down the path, making popping noises with his mouth to show that no person or animal was pulling him along.

Old Carz had, of course, many other tales for those who would listen. They were always about the Old Days by which, as he must have been about ninety, he meant the time of the Upheaval before the Foundation of our village: tales of people having a kind of box in which they could see what was happening miles away, and of getting their food not by growing it in the fields but miraculously producing it in a place he called "the shopz"; and of what he called a plane, which must have been some huge bird-like carz for people, he said, could fly in it. And, perhaps the most ridiculous tale of all, that the people of the time had been driven by some incomprehensible madness into rushing about and destroying such wonders. All this, he told, had happened in the Old Days; and he reckoned those to have ended in the year before the Foundation—which we spoke of as the First Year, but which he called by the numbers nineteen-ninety-seven. But few of us willingly listened to such stories; they were, we knew, the ramblings of an old man whose decaying mind befuddled his memories.

We were sure, then, that his tales were fantasies for we had the one about the Wall to gauge his reasoning by. The Wall that rose sharply above his hut had once, he told, reached right across the valley shutting off the upper pasture; and indeed there was on the far side another fragment of wall and between the two a great mass of tumbled stone which seemed at first glance to confirm his strange notion. But his explanation of the Wall—which he persisted in calling "the old dam"—made nonsense to us, nonsense by which we judged his other imaginings. He asserted that the middle part of the Wall had been blown away—"blown up" was the phrase he used—but, though in winter the wind sometimes howled down the valley and tore at our roofs, none of us could imagine a gale so fierce as to move such rocks as the Wall was made of. And he told, too, that the Wall had been built to hold back the water of the brook into a vast pond, an idea which, I remember, particularly angered Father Dennis on one occasion.

Father Dennis in his lumbering way had seized on the absurdity. "Why would anyone want to hold back the water?" he had demanded, heavily stressing each word. "There would be hundreds and hundreds of bucketfuls of it, far more than would be needed to get through the driest summer."

Old Carz' thin mouth had tightened, twisting into an almost contemptuous line. "It wasn't for the people in the valley," he said. "It was for the people in towns."

"A townz?" Father Dennis's contempt matched the old man's. "You'll be telling us again that so many people lived in a townz that they could never have grown their food. And anyway"—his voice took on a triumphant tone—"how could they have gotten the water to a townz? Did they put it in buckets and carry them there in a carz?"

Old Carz' eyes glinted angrily, and then dulled as if in despair. "You'll never understand," he muttered and hobbled back into his hut.

Father Dennis, assuming he had gotten the better of the old man, looked again at the little pile of turves—he had come to the hut to see that we children had left Old Carz a sufficient supply of fuel—and then strode off towards the village, muttering to himself that it was time the old man "was left." He must have forgotten that I had been with him for, when he stopped halfway along the path to look at the fields rising up on either side of the valley, I nearly bumped into him. The oats that year had come up thinly and Father Dennis looked at it sourly. "It looks as if we'll have a hard winter," he muttered, scratching his beard as if in annoyance; and I guessed that he was still thinking of Old Carz and of the possibility that, if food became scarce, the old man would have to "be left." "It has to be done," he added to me before he turned and strode on. "It's Rule Number Eight."

That made it, I knew, unquestionable. The Rules had been set down by the Founder at the Beginning. And the fact that Father Dennis was knowledgeable in the Rules —for in his young days he had been chosen to learn the Reading and Writing—gave his words authority. I did not, then, as far as I can remember, have any feeling of anxiety for Old Carz alone in his hut.

Up to that time I had had few occasions to see the old man, but about six months later I found myself having to go up to his hut. It was late in the year during the time after Harvest but before the winter set in, a slack time for us children for our village was ready for the onset of the cold weather and there remained little for us to do outdoors. One morning Carole, who usually took Old Carz' stores up to him, had said looking at Susan, "It's time you got into the way of things. You could take Old Carz' stores up."

Susan—she was a slight little thing, being only a week over eleven and scarcely up to Carole's rounded shoulder

—had said nothing and her thin, small face had shown no surprise.

"You'll have to do it soon," Carole went on, and we knew that she was already thinking of the time when she would be old enough to go into the Parents' House and Susan would be oldest girl in the Children's House.

Susan said quietly, "But that's a long time." The path to Old Carz' hut was uphill all the way, and the store sack would feel heavy by the time she got there.

"You've got to start some time," said Carole.

Susan knew that if Carole demanded that she went, there could be no arguing. Carole was oldest girl. But she forestalled Carole. She said, in that quiet tone of hers, "Has it got to be a girl?"

As she spoke she gave a flash of a glance sideways at Stephen, as if hoping he might offer. But he sat, big and stolid, staring into the fire.

Carole turned to him, her round eyes wide open at the idea, a smile swelling her cheeks. "Why not, Stephen?" she asked, her voice a tone softer than when she had spoken to Susan; and then, as he lifted his eyes in annoyed surprise, she added, disappointed, "Well, Gerald could go."

"Me?" I said, and I did not welcome going up to the old man's hut.

Stephen's look had lightened under Carole's gaze; and behind us young John, squatting before the fire, suppressed a laugh. No doubt he had read the appeal in Carole's look; no doubt he had seen in it more than the matter of taking up Old Carz' stores. Just before, Carole had been thinking of the time when she would be going to live in the Parents' House. When that time came Stephen, a month older than she and already showing the first wisps of his beard, would be old enough for her to ask for him. The appeal in her eyes had more to it than the subject of the moment.

Stephen responded—though perhaps uppermost in his mind was the thought that, as oldest boy, he had to assert himself. He said abruptly, "Yes, you go, Gerald."

I had to go. One of the Rules laid down that the oldest boy was in charge of all the boys in the Children's House. I remember I felt annoyed with Carole that she had got Stephen to follow her wishes. I felt annoyed, quite unfairly, with John, too; his laugh had seemed to urge Stephen on. But I went for the stores.

At the door of the Grandparents' House, Grandmother Ruth was waiting. "You're taking it up?" she asked in sharp surprise, the lines on her thin, wrinkled face seeming to deepen. She clicked her tongue. "That Carole! She'll get out of anything. Well, we'll see when she's got a baby or two to think of. Perhaps she'll learn then that work's got to be done. . . . And tell him," she added, with a nod towards Old Carz' sack of provisions, "to make it last. The winter's ahead of us and we can't expect as kind a one as last."

I took up the sack and started along the path. At first the going was easy; the path kept to the gentle slope beside the brook. In one of the fields that reached up towards the Mountain, the Fathers were working at the autumn plowing, Father Dennis guiding the plow while Father Timothy and Father Alan dragged it along through the stony earth. Above them Grandfather Tony and Grandfather Brian were repairing the field wall. That was a usual autumn work for, though the field walls were ancient and strong, we could never be sure that during the hungry winter the rabbits and wild pigs, driven by the dogs in the forest on the far side of the Mountain, would not find a way through to the sprouting grain next spring.

Beyond the highest field the way became rough. It rose more steeply as it approached the Wall and for thirty or so paces it was all but blocked by great slabs of stone, not the stone of the field walls but of a lighter-colored, smoother stone similar to that of the Wall itself. They sprawled across the valley between the two fragments of Wall; if it had been possible to accept Old Carz' story about the Wall being blown down, they could have been the remains of the missing middle. But then I was more concerned to clamber through the stone slabs than to puzzle about their origin, for the path twisted and turned among the tangle of growth that had long ago sprung up about them. And I wanted to deliver the old man's stores and get back as quickly as I could. I would not have admitted to being afraid of him, but I felt through my tunic for the shrill whistle hanging from my neck that all of us carried to summon help if we got into any difficulty or saw a stranger, human or animal, in the valley. I did not expect to use it, but it was a comfort to feel the whistle as I drew near to Old Carz' hut.

The old man opened the door while I was still a dozen paces away. He stood, his twisted foot slightly lifted, his eyes under their jutting brows glinting, though whether in annoyance or welcome I could not tell.

"Where's the girl?" he asked. "Is she sick?"

"No," I said. I did not try to explain why Carole had not come; I could see it would involve me in a conversation with him, and I had no wish for that.

His look shifted to the sack of provisions. "Put it inside," he said.

That was the first time I had been into the hut. It was, as I expected, sufficient and plain: just large enough for a board bed along one side and a table and a stool along the other and, between, the hearth. I remember wondering, as I put the stores on the table, what it was like to live up there alone, apart from the rest of us. I supposed that one day, when I became too old to work, I would know, but that was a long time off.

As I turned to go out, Old Carz said with a glance at the bucket standing just inside the door, "I'll be wanting water."

"All right," I said.

I went to the spring across the upper pasture. It was quite a walk, and first I had to negotiate more huge slabs of stone which thereabouts were so overgrown with brambles and bushes that I soon realized it would have been easier to go down to where, long ago, a gap had been made near the brook to allow the cattle to be driven to and from the upper pasture. Indeed, after I had filled the old man's bucket at the spring oozing slightly brown from the mountain turf, I came back the easier way so as not to spill too much. All told, it took me perhaps a half hour to go to the spring and back to the hut.

Old Carz must have been noticing the time, for he asked with a hint of surprise softening his rasping voice, "You've been to the spring?"

"Yes," I said, and for a moment did not realize that Carole, to save the walk, must have taken to refilling his bucket from the nearer brook.

He nodded; and then, before I could begin on my way down to the village, "You're Alan's boy, aren't you?"

The question surprised me though, to be sure, it was like the old man to phrase it in such a way. Ordinarily we children did not speak of particular parents; all the men and women in the Parents' House we thought of collectively as the Parents. Among them we knew each of us had a mother and a father, but we did not think of a particular pair as being ours. That Mother Rachel was my mother must have been the earliest of memories, but I had little memory of Father Alan as my father. Like the other men he had spent most of his time out in the fields and had only come into the Parents' House at dusk along with the other Fathers so that, during the few years I had lived there before being transferred to the Children's House, he had seemed to me merely one of the Fathers. But recently Grandmother Ruth, hard-eyed and ever watchful, had commented that I was coming to look more like Alan every day. Grandmother Mary, who had been sitting with her at the Grandparents' House door at the time, had looked a little shocked, as if Grandmother Ruth should not have so spoken in my hearing; and in that look, as much as in what Grandmother Ruth had said, I read that Alan was my father. I had felt almost guilty, as if I had overheard talk about things I should not know.

It was like Old Carz to overlook or defy the niceties of the Parents in such matters. Without waiting for my answer, he went on, "Yes, you'll be Alan's. You have the look of him about you."

Hoping to get away before he said more, I asked if there was anything else he was needing.

He did not answer. Instead he went on with his own thoughts. "Alan should have been taught the Reading and the Writing. He'd have made more of it than Dennis will ever do." He shot a sideways glance at me. "If you're chosen to learn the Reading and Writing, come and tell me," he said.

His request—for there was a softness in his voice which hinted of asking rather than of commanding—surprised me. I could not then understand why he should have shown such interest in me or in the village doings, for ever since I could remember he had lived far up the valley, apart from the rest of us. And probably I felt flattered by his suggestion that I might be chosen to learn the Readings and Writing. I had assumed that Stephen would be chosen; he was oldest boy and I had come to expect that he would always take preference over me. And yet the old man thought that I might be chosen, and that, in turn, implied the possibility that I might one day become the

Headman for, of course, only one who had the skills of Reading and Writing, and therefore knew the Rules, could be chosen as the village's ruler.

Old Carz must have watched my face and read something of the feelings his request had prompted—though he could not have guessed that for me the most important was the possibility of becoming in time over Stephen. He went on, "You'll be chosen most likely. You're not that strong yet that your work will be missed on the heavy tasks. Peter will choose you if he has any sense . . . and perhaps you would be able to understand. You won't understand it all, not at first; but when you've read through my book you'll begin to know."

"Your book?" I asked. The word was unknown to me then.

"My writings!" he said sharply. "Writings make a book, pages of them, all I can remember. I'm going to write it all down." And then, misinterpreting my alarm for interested surprise, he went on, "You'll understand more than that Dennis will ever begin to know. He'll never understand how people, far more people than he's ever thought of, lived together in towns and, instead of growing their own food—"

At the word "townz" I became more uneasy for he was clearly starting on one of his rambling stories. Soon he would be building fantasy on fantasy until he was telling of people being able to hear what was said miles away, and flying in the air.

He misread my expression. "But you've seen one," he

went on, his darkly-hooded eyes seeming to lighten. "You must have, when you were up on the Mountain."

I did not understand. "There isn't a townz up there," I ventured. There was, I knew, only the ridge running level under the sky except for the hollow where the Fathers cut the turf, and beyond that, down the far slope, the forest reaching out.

"There is! Over that way!" And he pointed a bony, twisted finger towards the far end of the ridge.

And I remembered. It must have been the year before when some of the sheep had wandered off along the ridge and Father Harold, who had been acting shepherd that day, had whistled us up on the Mountain to help search for them. Stephen and I went farther along the ridge than I had ever been before, on to where, almost at the ridge end, we could see a valley far wider than ours reaching out. It was thick with trees but, being early spring at the time, we made out what looked like clearings in the forest with wisps of smoke rising from them. They must, I knew, be other villages, for Smith when he called to repair our tools and utensils, sometimes told the Grandparents of the places he visited in his wanderings, places which in my imagination were villages much like ours.

One particular break in the forest had caught my gaze. It looked like a patch of rock; it was far away and hard to make out, but the rock did not appear so haphazard as that about our valley. It looked more like buildings of stone.

"What can it be?" I had asked Stephen.

"Some old rocks," he had said incuriously.

"It looks more like houses," I had said, puzzled.

He gave a shrug. "It can't be houses. There's too many of them. Where would the people grow their food?"

I had accepted his explanation for, like him, I could not imagine people living in so large a village that they would not have enough land to grow their own food. And, as far as I could see, the forest reached right up to the patch of rock, intruded among it in places; there was little hint of open space, of fields, about it.

Old Carz' pointing finger reminded me of the sight.

"You mean those old rocks?" I asked, "the rocks out in the forest?"

"Have you been there?" he asked, his tone taking on a hint of urgency. "Have you seen the place close to?" And then, as I did not respond, he added, "Of course you're not allowed to go and see . . . but there are houses there, thousands of them."

"Thousands?" I asked, not knowing the word.

"Hundreds and hundreds," he explained. "And people: they lived there once, as many people as . . ." He hesitated, looking around for some way of telling me how many. "You see that tree?" he asked, pointing down the valley. "No, not that bare one! The holly: how many leaves are there on it, do you think?"

The question sounded unanswerable. "Hundreds and hundreds," I ventured as I tried to think of some excuse to get away from him.

"Thousands and more than thousands," he said. "And

there were once as many people in that town, or in towns like it. In London there were millions, and in Birmingham and Manchester and Liverpool, too."

The names meant nothing to me and I would probably have forgotten them if I had not heard them again when I was being considered for the Reading and Writing. But that was still in the future. Then, at Old Carz' hut, I thought they were fantasies of extreme age, woven out of slight threads of memories. It seemed utterly impossible that there could have been collections of houses large enough for more than a hundred people. The two dozen of us had to work all our time to produce enough in our valley, and we needed but the three Houses to live in. A townz large enough to house a hundred people would need far larger fields.

My disbelief must have shown on my face and this time Old Carz read my look rightly.

"Of course you're kept from knowing," he said, his tone gentler and the glint in his eyes fading. "But one day you could understand. And when I've written it all down, all I can remember, and you're chosen for the Reading and Writing, you come and tell me."

Again I felt the compliment of his assumption, and a trace of pride at the possibility that, one day, I might be over Stephen.

"All right," I said, probably a little carelessly.

That seemed to end the conversation, but as I turned away he asked, "Is that a promise?"

"All right," I said again, and then I was off.

I had no idea then what the old man was expecting of me. All I can remember is that once, as I scrambled over a slab of rock and nearly fell, I happened to glance back at the hut. The old man was still at the door, watching me, and on his leathery face was a look of mingled hope and uncertainty. Unexpectedly he waved. I was so surprised that I waved back before I ran on.

The Headman

I DID NOT for some days give much thought to what Old
Carz had said. I had seen that he had expected me to
believe him; and I had been flattered by his assumption
that I would be chosen for the Reading and Writing. Perhaps it was that which caused some of his phrases to lodge
in my mind. "You're kept from knowing," he had said,
and when referring to the townz he said was beyond the
Mountain: "Of course you're not allowed to go and see."

At that time I had not begun to realize how restricted
was our life in the valley. It was, after all, the only way
of living that any of us but the old man had known. Of
course we knew that beyond the Mountain other people
lived; Smith had told of them when he called to repair

our few iron tools, and our men when out hunting sometimes met other hunters; and now and again a pedlar
called, selling salt or trying to interest the Mothers in
some bright thin cloth, or a traveller who had lost his
way might come down the valley. Such contacts, few
though they were, had kept us aware that other peoples
lived in the forest that stretched out from the far side
of our Mountain and below where the valley was choked
with the tangle of trees and brambles and humps of earth
that we called the Waste. When I thought about such
people I assumed them to live much as we did: in groups
of three or four long one-roomed houses, with everyone
living communally in their generations, and surrounded
by the fields and pastures in which they produced their
food and other necessities.

This very limited outlook had arisen largely from the
circumstances which had led to our living in the valley.
We all knew the outline of the story, like a fairy tale it was
passed on to each of us in childhood. About eighty years
earlier, we were told, there had been a great Upheaval
among the people then living. A kind of madness had
taken hold of them so that they went about burning and
destroying and stealing from one another, until so little
food could be grown that people starved in the hundreds. So terrible had been that time that villages, even
the largest of them, had become deserted. The houses
had fallen into ruin, the animals had wandered off to
become in time the wild ones we sometimes hunted, and
forest had crept over the once-productive fields.

It was during the Upheaval that the Founder had come

to our valley. He had brought with him five children, two boys and three girls, of whom his nephew Paul—now Old Carz to us—had been the youngest; the others, so the story told, he had found on the journey. In the seclusion of the valley he had begun the creation of our village, the five children learning under his guidance how to tend animals, how to grow the oats and potatoes and the vegetables, how to build the Houses that were now our homes, and how to live together.

In my imagination the Founder was an austere figure, white-bearded and stern. I have learnt that he was, in fact, slight and small, and had been by occupation a vet, from which sprang the farming skills and the medical knowledge that were passed down to us. He had died in his forties, though by then our first generation—the Great-grandparents—were themselves parents and the little community could survive.

The manner of the Founder's death must have had a great effect on our development. We all knew the story of how the house had caught fire and the Founder had been killed when a burning beam fell on him as he tried to save what we came to call his Writings. The event seemed to invest the Writings with some strange and sinister power, though the skills of reading and writing were not wholly lost, indeed, every ten years or so, one of the boys was chosen to learn them so that there would be at least one in each generation who could, when the need arose, pronounce the Rules. But writings other than the Rules had come to be regarded as suspect; they had caused the Founder's death and, so it was told, had turned

Grandfather Philip's mind so that he would not work and eventually, in a fit of madness, had blundered into the Forbidden Area and disappeared mysteriously.

I think it probable that among the Founder's writings destroyed in the fire were books other than those on veterinary subjects which would have given us some awareness of how people had lived before the Upheaval. As it was, our knowledge of the world beyond our valley was limited to the stories that had been passed from parents to children, and those were of happenings since the Foundation. Otherwise we had nothing . . . except for what were whispered about as "the Documents." These were said to be fragments of old writing that had been found casually about the village in the early days. Perhaps because the Founder's successor as Headman, Great-grandfather Robert, had thought them of significance, these "Documents" had been preserved, but they were not public property. Only to those who were chosen to learn the Reading and Writing were they ever shown. Kept in the privacy of the Headman's room, they were believed to tell of the Upheaval, to describe in fearsome vividness the events of that time so terrible that it was still spoken of in hushed voices and, at least before us children, with reluctance.

Such was the impression we had acquired—though when the Headman took the first step in choosing the next Learner of the Reading and Writing, I began to glimpse a little of the reality behind such passed-on knowledge.

It must have been about ten days after I had first taken

up Old Carz' stores when the Headman, Grandfather
Peter, came into our House. Ordinarily the Grandparents
seldom came to the Children's House; our visitors were
one or other of the Parents who came to tell us what sup-
plies to collect from the barn, what work we had to do, or
to see that the House was tidy and clean. Grandfather
Peter's coming was an event. I remember that Carole,
who must have been warned a few minutes in advance,
had us all scurrying around, tidying our bunks and clearing away the ashes that had spilled over the hearth and
sweeping any dried mud out of sight. And then, suddenly, the door opened and the Headman strode in.

We all stood still. Grandfather Peter paused in the
center of the House, in the space between door and fire.
He stood a full head taller than Stephen, gaunt and hunch-
shouldered with his head held slightly bent so that his
straggling beard almost rested on his chest, a formidable
figure even without the status of Headman. As he paused,
a turf fell in the fire and a sudden glow lit up his face,
catching the big jutting nose, the high cheekbones and
the thin, tight line of his mouth; but the glow seemed not
to reach into the small eyes set deep in their sockets.

He gave only the slightest glance towards the girls
though Carole's full face, flushed from her exertions, was
turned towards him perhaps in expectation of favorable
comment. Nor did he seem to notice little Patrick who
had struggled to his feet and was thrusting out his stomach
in an attempt to stand appropriately stiffly.

The little sharp eyes turned first to the oldest of us
boys.

"Stephen?" Grandfather Peter asked, almost as a command.

"Yes," grunted Stephen.

"And John?" There was a hint of puzzlement as if he had not realized that John was younger than I.

His usual smile wavering, John could only nod.

The Headman's eyes turned to me. "You're Gerald, aren't you?"

Something in his tone, a trace of curiosity perhaps, seemed to suggest that in some way he had already singled me out from the others.

Dry mouthed, I managed to answer, "Yes."

It was, of course, the first time I had been involved in the choosing. I had imagined that the occasion might be marked with some slight ceremony, the chosen Learner receiving special acknowledgement. I remember feeling myself go tense in the long moment while we waited for the Headman's pronouncement, but to my disappointment he abruptly ordered the three of us to follow him to the Grandparents' House before he turned to the door. We walked in file, Stephen leading, me following, and John, looking far from easy, at the end as the youngest. I expect that the Grandparents, sitting around their fire or on their wall beds, watched us with interest; but I was aware only of the trembling of my legs and, ahead of us, the door of Grandfather Peter's room, a secret place, for only the Headman had the distinction of a room to himself.

The sight of the Headman's room did something to

lessen my apprehensions and also my disappointment at the terse indifference with which Grandfather Peter seemed to be regarding what we had come to believe was a momentous occasion. I think I must have expected some of the mysterious Writing to be on display or at least some indication that the room had witnessed the Learning and the passing on of the secret knowledge that only the Headman possessed. But it was a small room, scarcely larger than Old Carz' hut, and it had an ordinary, lived-in appearance. The top of the little table was worn from long use and stained where food had been spilled, and the stool was no different, except in size, from those we had in the Children's House. The only unusual feature was the pair of shelves along one wall on which lay some thin boards, and on those dust lingered.

Grandfather Peter squirmed his long, bent-shouldered body round the table and sat on the stool facing us. But his face, now nearer our level, did not look more sympathetic. For a long moment his little eyes darted from one to another of us. He must have seen from our startled looks that he needed to put us a little at ease before explaining why he had brought us there for, I remember, a smile twisted his tight mouth as he began to explain. One of us was to learn the Reading and Writing that winter: the question was, which one?

He went on talking and though I made every effort to follow his words, something about the man and the occasion seemed to persist in intruding. Again and again I found myself almost desperately trying to cling to what he was saying, trying to snatch at a phrase or two and hold its meaning before the next sentence came to elude me. I know he impressed on us the need for secrecy; anything that we saw then or when we were learning must be kept to ourselves alone, and not even discussed between us. Only when the time came for whichever of us was chosen to pass on our learning to the next Learner—and that would be most of a generation's time away—could we divulge the secret knowledge, and then only to the next chosen.

"You three are of an age to become Learner," he went on and, with a glance at Stephen, "That is, if you can learn quickly. It may be that you will not have much time. The winter may be mild and not keep us indoors much." It seemed that we were expected to master the mysteries of the Reading and Writing in half days when outdoor work was impossible, a notion that, having for so long believed the skills beyond the understanding of any but a select few, bewildered me. "Well," he concluded, "let's see what you think of it."

He turned and with a long arm took a few of the thin boards from a shelf and held one out to each of us. They were of a thinness and smoothness that I had never seen before; indeed I doubted if Grandfather Tony, who was reckoned the best woodworker in the village, could have made anything so fine. On them groups of signs had been drawn in black. They were arranged in rows and I noticed that every second or third row began with the same little group of four signs. It was, of course, the first time that any of us had ever seen writing.

Grandfather Peter looked up from the similar board on his table to watch our faces.

"Puzzling, isn't it?" he asked, an unexpected hint of amusement in his tone. "Those signs make words—words you say. That first word—at the top to the left—that says 'Rule.' After that comes the word for 'One.' So it starts: 'Rule One.' Do you get the idea?"

He had asked Stephen, but Stephen made no reply. He stared in scowling bewilderment at his board.

"You're holding it upside down," said Grandfather Peter drily.

He glanced at me.

I had had a moment to look at my board. I had discovered a little group of shapes three lines lower than the beginning but like the first word. Pointing at it I ventured, "Is that 'Rule Two?' "

The Headman's surprise sounded genuine. "That's good," he said. "That's very good—er, Gerald." He turned to John. "Can you find where it says 'Rule Three?' " he asked.

The Headman must have seemed an even more fearsome being to eight-year-old John than he was to me. John's eyes searched down the line, his usual smile utterly banished. At last, almost in desperation, he pointed at a word. It was not, I already knew, "Rule Three."

For the next few minutes Grandfather Peter tried us again and again. He would tell us to look at a line while he said the words; then we had to try and find which shape fitted which word. Stephen persisted in being baffled and I felt a tingling of pride creeping over me when, most times, I found the word. I felt a little sorry for John, though. He did find a few words, but I knew that I had done better.

Grandfather Peter leaned back on his stool and again regarded us. "Well, that's given you a little idea of the Reading," he said. "And it's given me something to work on. When the time comes, I'll have a better idea of who to choose. Let me have your Rule boards."

We handed them back and he picked up the one he had been looking at to return them all to the shelf; and then we noticed that he had taken down a fifth board, a very different one from those we had just been shown. The signs on it were not drawn directly on to the wood; they had been made on a thin, yellowish sheet which covered the board. The word shapes were much smaller and neater than those we had been looking at; and above them were what I have since learned are called pictures. They were made in shades of gray, and showed people dressed in strange costumes: a smiling girl, old enough to be a Mother, wearing only a single close-fitting garment that left her arms and legs so bare that she would have scratched herself if she had walked only a few paces along a path, let alone joined in the Harvest work; and a group of beardless men, dressed in trews so short that they would have been useless for working in the fields, apparently running after a round object.

All three of us stared at the board in amazement. Grandfather Peter smiled.

"You'll not have seen anything like that," he said, pointing at the board. "That's paper!"

I assumed that he was referring to the strange kind of board.

"It's an old document," he went on, "from the time of the Upheaval. There aren't many of them left." He pointed to the row of larger signs along the tattered top of the paper. "It's the AILY MIRR," he explained, "an old record they kept in those days. It tells of the Upheaval. It says there"—and he pointed to a line of signs lower down—" 'MORE BOMB OUTRAGES' and that says: 'RIOTING AT DOCKS ADDS TO FOOD SHORTAGES.' "

I was still staring at the strange picture of the men running after the round thing. Grandfather Peter caught my gaze. "That's a picture of one of the many battles of that terrible time," he said. He pointed a long finger at the round object. "That's a bomb. You'll not know about bombs. They were dangerous. They—they—" He seemed to have difficulty in remembering a word—"they burst suddenly, killing people and knocking down buildings. They had many of them in the Old Days."

I could not imagine how the thing he called a bomb could hurt anyone, and the men in the picture appeared to be running towards it rather than away from it. John and Stephen also found the picture puzzling. As if aware of our puzzlement, Grandfather Peter went on, pointing at some rows of small signs lower down the board: "There are records of some of the battles they fought. Let me see if I can remember them. That one says 'Bradford v Spurs,' and that's 'Everton v Huddersfield,' and that one's 'Chelsea v Liverpool,' and that's—"

"Liverpool!" I had blurted out the word before I recalled where I had heard it. Old Carz had said it was a townz.

Grandfather Peter jerked his head up to stare at me, his eyes suddenly sharp and suspicious, the smile gone from his lips.

"Where have you heard of 'Liverpool?' " he demanded.

I had to say something. I stammered, "I—it was a townz, wasn't it?"

I knew immediately that I had said the wrong thing. For a long moment the Headman sat glaring at me, his little eyes seeming to pierce into my thoughts. At last he said, "You've been listening to too many old fools' tales."

He flung the board on to the shelf and said abruptly, "I'll let you know whom I choose."

As I followed the others out of the room, I felt convinced that I had lost any chance to be next Learner. My blundering reference to "Liverpool" had so obviously angered him that Grandfather Peter would dismiss me as unsuitable. He might even think that if he allowed me to learn the Reading and Writing it would turn my brain as it had turned Grandfather Philip's long ago.

So when the next morning I went up again to Old Carz' hut I said nothing of my being one of those from whom the next Learner was to be chosen. Indeed I felt, as I toiled up the path, even more depressed for that morning Stephen had been sharply commanding—prompted perhaps by his poor showing at the Reading—and my hope that one day I would be able to order him about had all but vanished.

It was a sunny morning, one of those days when au-

tumn seems determined not to give way to winter, and
the old man was sitting at the open door. He had before
him the table on which were some sheets of whitish stuff,
and in his hand he held a thin reed which he must have
gone down to the brook to cut. As I reached him I noticed that the tip of the reed was black from a paste of
soot and water that he had on the table. With it he had
been making signs on the sheet before him, though they
were smaller and tighter than those I had seen on the
Headman's boards, I guessed that they were Old Carz'
idea of the Writing. But though I started at the sight,
it did not stir my curiosity, rather, it added to my feeling
of failure.

He must have been waiting for me. He seemed pleased
to see me. Unaware of my despondency he said, pointing
a bony finger at the sheet, "You won't know what that is.
It's paper."

"Paper?" It didn't look much like the board Grandfather Peter had called paper.

"There are only a few sheets of it left," the old man
went on, his tone almost excited. "We've lost the way of
making it. And that"—he pointed to the marks he had
made—"do you know what that is?"

I did, though it looked small and insignificant beside
the Writing I had seen in the Headman's room.

"Yes," I said. "It's the Writing."

I probably spoke irritably, but at the same time I was
ready to show my new knowledge. I remember that the
old man's eyes flashed to my face.

"So you've been chosen!" he exclaimed.

His tone with its unexpected hopefulness caught me. For a moment I glimpsed something of his thoughts: the hope that one day I would be able to read his writings, would come to understand what he believed—fantastic though it sounded to us. And, recalling Grandfather Peter's anger when he had guessed how I had known of "Liverpool," I nearly blurted out that I wasn't likely to be chosen. One part of me wanted not to become involved with the old man, not to risk more of the Headman's sharp disapproval, but Old Carz' look, near to appealing, checked me. I said only, "No, I haven't been chosen."

Disappointment stole the brightness from his old eyes. "But the writing," he began uncertainly. "How did you know it if? . . ."

"Grandfather Peter's going to choose later," I said, and then, seeing his empty bucket, I snatched it up and escaped to the spring.

I was in a tangle of feeling. I wished—I did not know why—I could tell the old man that I might be chosen, and yet I was afraid of his delighted reaction. I guessed that Old Carz wanted to tell me something; I knew that I dared not listen. I wished to know, to understand, but I was afraid of where knowledge might lead. I remember that, as I paused a moment on the way up to the spring, I looked back down the valley, our valley. In the mellow October sunlight it looked quiet and safe, protected by the rising mountains and by the tangle of the Waste that blocked the lower end. And at the same moment I remembered Old Carz' words when he had told of the townz. "Of course you're not allowed to go and see," and I felt a twinge of curiosity about what lay beyond the Mountain. And then my eyes caught sight of the others—Stephen and John, Carole and Susan—little figures but recognizable at that distance, down near the Waste. They were, I knew, going in search of the nuts and berries which we always laid in for the winter, but they were, as usual, making for the eastern side of the Waste. To the west, where a spur of the Mountain jutted out to narrow the valley, was the Forbidden Area.

When later I recalled that moment, the sight seemed to have something symbolic about it: the two parts of the Waste, one familiar, its woods providing necessary fruits and timber, the other, appearing merely an extension, and yet prohibited to us. Of course I knew the story that hung about the Forbidden Area: how Grandfather Philip, his mind turned by the Reading and Writing, had after long weeks of moody silences suddenly stridden off into the Forbidden Area almost as an act of defiance; and how some had gone after him—Grandfather Peter had been one, and Grandmother Mary, too—and had been startled by a great, wild cry; and when at last they ventured into the Area they had found no sign of Grandfather Philip. It was as if with that last fearful cry Grandfather Philip had vanished, as if—so the story ended—the earth had swallowed him.

The story was in my mind as I toiled to the spring. It told only too clearly of the danger of not accepting, of venturing beyond the known limits of the valley, beyond our way of living. Outside our protecting Mountain and Waste was a strange and fearful world in which unexplained things had happened . . . and in which, according to Old Carz' tales, people had lived impossibly.

When I got back with the spring water, I found the old man waiting for me. He had, in the interval, apparently revived his conviction that I would be chosen for the Reading and Writing. As I put down the bucket, he took up a sheet of his writing and said, "You're not in a hurry, are you? I'll read you a little of what I've written."

I stared my alarm. If ever the Headman came to hear that I had listened to Old Carz' writings, I would be regarded almost as an outcast.

But the old man had already begun, " 'The time will come when we will regain the knowledge we have lost, but we must never again allow that knowledge to master us. Our inventions must be kept within our control and never allowed to shape our lives so that we come to destroy what we have created. As we must learn to use explosives not to destroy life but to help with necessary work, so we must not use our cars to dominate—' "

"Carz!" I seized on the word, almost the only one I had understood. It seemed, in that moment, to give me a decision. The things the old man talked of—and was now writing about—belonged only in his aging imagination. I could not, I dared not, think of believing in them. That way led to untold dangers, perhaps even to the madness that had driven Grandfather Philip to his mysterious end in the Forbidden Area.

The old man had lifted his head to stare at me. I knew without meeting his eyes that they held disappointment, perhaps bitterness. He believed he knew greath truths; I, like all of us, was rejecting them, was clinging to the safe familiar thoughts rather than risk venturing into the unknown.

"I—it's no good!" I stammered. "I'll never be chosen." And I ran away, scrambled hurriedly over the boulders, scratching and cutting myself in my haste to be away from him, back down the valley.

I ran on past the Houses. I felt I had to join Carole and Stephen and the others, to keep within the known ways.

I found them quickly enough in the curiously humped and overgrown ground we called the Waste. As I had guessed, they were picking nuts and late berries. Carole and Stephen were a little apart and seemed to be talking together rather than searching. John was reaching for the nuts five-year-old Patrick had found with pride. Susan was telling little Angela to leave alone the deadly night-shade, tempting though its purple berries looked.

I joined Susan. Ordinarily I would have gone with John but he was involved in the Reading and Writing, and I did not want to think more about them. Susan, always quiet, was not likely to ask questions, to stir my churning thoughts.

Seeing me, she gave a quick flash of a look as if to say that I had stayed overlong with Old Carz.

I muttered, "He started talking."

I had misjudged Susan. Her quietness of manner, I was to learn, masked thoughts that went far beyond what the rest of us yet knew. As I began searching for hazelnuts, she asked, "What about?"

"His usual old tales," I said, edging away.

Susan followed, though seeming only to be looking for fruits. I realized afterwards that she had waited until even little Angela was out of hearing before she asked, "Did he talk about a carz?"

Such persistence was, I thought, unlike her and in my present mood it irritated me. I wanted to forget the old man and the hopefulness that I had heard in his voice, his clinging to the possibility that I would, in time, come to read his writings with their absurd notions.

I replied shortly, "Oh yes. He always does."

I was aware that Susan glanced back towards the others before she spoke again.

She said, "I've seen one."

I thought for a moment that she was meaning a fruit or a hazelnut.

"It's over there," she added, nodding ahead of us.

I stared at her as I understood. I did not believe that she could have actually seen a carz; she must have mistaken some tangle of brambles and a fallen tree perhaps. I blurted out, "But that's the Forbidden Area! What if someone had seen you?"

She replied calmly, "No one did . . . and it was a carz. I'll take you there when we get the chance."

"What! Into the Forbidden Area!"

Carole heard my voice though she could not have caught the words. She and Stephen turned towards us. "You two!" Carole called. "You aren't working!"

Susan whispered, "It's rotted away quite a lot. But it was made of iron—or something like it. And it had wheels."

Carole, with Stephen coming along behind her, was too near for Susan to risk saying more. She reached for a cluster of rose hips.

"I should think so!" said Carole. "We didn't come out to chat!" Perhaps awareness of her own and Stephen's loitering added near-adult disapproval to her tone.

Stephen followed her lead. He turned on me: "And you spent long enough up at Old Carz.' If you're that long again, I'll tell the Headman."

Susan did not say more about what she had seen and had assumed to be a carz. Living together in the one House, we children rarely had opportunities to talk together without others hearing. Until then it had not troubled me; it was part of our normal way of living that we all knew what the others were doing and saying. And we usually worked as a group; if we were paired for some task, Stephen's strength was usually supplemented by Susan's slightness while Carole and I worked together. So, if I had wanted to, I could not easily have questioned Susan about what she had seen, and I was not sure that I wanted to. The fact that she had been to the Forbidden Area alarmed me for myself as well as for her. I imagined that if it ever became known, some terrible punishment would befall her, and if it were known that I had learned that she had been there and had not told the Headman I, too, would be in trouble.

Such fears went with me to my bunk that night. Long

after easy-going John and little Patrick across the House had ceased to stir, long after Stephen on the bunk above me had fallen asleep, I lay staring into the darkness. My mind, between thinking and dreaming, pictured Susan scrambling about in the Forbidden Area, becoming entangled in the brambles, in huge brambles that rose monstrously all around her, clutching her, seizing her, dragging her down under a massive tree trunk that was being moved along by great curving bramble stems like a carz—

I jerked suddenly wide awake. Not until then had I fully realized what Susan had told me. My fears about her going to the Forbidden Area had blotted out what she said she had found there. My mind snatched at the recollection. What if she had seen a carz? What if there was really such a thing, if what Old Carz told was true? I felt as I had felt that morning, torn between a wish to know and a fear of what knowledge might bring.

I recalled the old man on my first visit pointing his bony finger over the far end of the Mountain, his talk of a townz being there, of hundreds and hundreds of people living in it. What if it was so, or had been so in the days before the Upheaval? Perhaps there really had been much larger villages than ours, perhaps the people had known things that we in our confining valley had never dreamed of....

I tried to visualize a larger village than ours, with perhaps a hundred people in it. It would need a wider valley and one with richer soil than our small, rocky fields provided. But a townz such as Old Carz had told of, so crammed with people that it would need fields stretching to the horizon to feed them all—that was impossible. Perhaps, when he was a boy and the Founder had brought him and the other Great-grandparents to the refuge of our valley, he had passed through a large village and now, an old man no longer able to work and having time only to think back to that distant past, he was enlarging his memory of that village into a monstrous townz without realizing that a place so huge could never have had land enough to provide for its needs.

It was a comforting explanation, and soon I was asleep.

The Pale Strangers

IT WAS NOT UNTIL after our second hunting that I determined to ask Susan about what she believed she had seen in the Forbidden Area. I think now that fear must have kept me from asking her, but had it been possible for me to forget what she had told me, she would not have let me. Ever and again I caught her glance, the eyes with just the hint of a smile in them, her eyebrows slightly lifted in question, and I knew that she was wondering when I would ask her to show me whatever she had seen. I did not, yet, really believe it to have been a carz for I had grown up knowing that such a thing existed only in Old Carz' imagination. But on our second hunting John and I had an adventure which made me wonder if there could be some reality underlying the old man's improbable tales.

In the late autumn the Fathers went on hunts to supplement our winter stores. They hunted any likely game: rabbits they could be fairly sure of catching and perhaps a few wild chickens, but they always hoped to get on the trail of pigs or sheep or cattle that had strayed at the time of the Upheaval to become wild. Pigs were particularly sought for, bacon and pork made welcome changes to the beef or mutton we salted down for the winter. Once, it was said, we had kept pigs, but disease had killed them off back in the days when the Grandparents were young. There was occasional talk about trying to catch a few young ones and refounding our herd, but nothing came of it; we rarely had more fodder than was needed for the cattle we kept through the winter.

Stephen, being oldest boy, had already gone hunting in earlier autumns; for John and me the expeditions were exciting novelties. We set out one morning armed with knives and large clubs; we did not set traps for fear the wild dogs would get our prey before we did. We boys did not go with the main hunt; that was composed only of Fathers and was expected to go farther afield, perhaps even to stay the night in the forest. John and I were, as yet, only beginners, and we went with Stephen and Grandfather Tony who in his younger days had been reckoned our most skilled hunter.

Though John and I enjoyed the outing and the hopefulness of our first day's hunt, it was not in fact very rewarding. Grandfather Tony, a wizened, nervous little man always ready to expect the worst, led us only to the lower slopes of the far side of the Mountain, to the fringe of the forest that stretched out over a wider valley than ours. There we tried our luck at catching rabbits. We repaired the cages of sticks made on earlier hunts about some of their holes, and then, after hiding nearby for what seemed a very long time, we chased such rabbits as had ventured out and tried to stun them with our clubs before they could penetrate the blocked entrances to their burrows. Stephen was the most successful of us. He got four rabbits, John and I only one each. Grandfather Tony, no longer nimble enough to join in the killing, contented himself with telling us what to do and watching while we tried to do it.

Before our second hunt, two days later, I realized that I had on that first day not taken the opportunity to see much of the strange land that reached out beyond our Mountain. The excitement of the hunt had overlain my recollection of Old Carz telling of a townz being visible from the far end of the Mountain and we had, in truth, scarcely ventured more than a few hundred paces from familiar ground. But as we set out a second time, I resolved to be on the watch for any signs of what the old man had hinted.

I assumed that our second hunt would follow much the same pattern as the first and that while we were waiting to catch rabbits on the far slope, I would be able to glimpse any telltale signs in the unfamiliar forest below us. But even before we had begun to look for fresh rab-

bit burrows, Stephen spotted the new trail of pig. We
boys assumed at once that we would track the pig—
though Grandfather Tony, when he saw that the trail led
downwards into the forest, was inclined to discourage
us. Timorous and unsure as ever, he followed rather than
led us when Stephen started off along the trail.

Stephen reckoned that we were following a small herd,
and the tracks persisted down into the forest far enough
for Grandfather Tony to become anxious—although it
was not yet midday and, looking back through the bare
branches, we could still clearly see the Mountain and the
way home. As we went on I noticed a tangle of rusted
iron, once some kind of structure but long ago grown
over with crowding bushes. We made cuts on the trees
nearby to mark the place for we knew that Smith, when
he called at our village, often asked the Grandparents
where the precious metal could be found; it was said that
sometimes when he had repaired our tools he had taken
the whereabouts of a good supply of iron as part payment. Further on, after scrambling over what might once
have been the stone wall to a field, we came upon the ruin
of a small house strangely divided into rooms that were
little bigger than Old Carz' hut, and which we saw from
the new ashes in one corner had been sheltered in recently. Grandfather Tony called it "a bad place," and
wanted to turn back, but Stephen had found the pigs'
trail going on beyond . . . and so, in only a few paces,
we came out on a curious path making its way through
the forest.

It was smooth and made not of earth or stones but of a

leathery, blackish stuff. There was, we all knew, a brief stretch of similar trackway in our valley, a mere half-dozen paces that disappeared under the hummocky ground of the Waste. But this stretch of trackway went on in either direction as far as we could see.

The sight made Grandfather Tony more uneasy than ever. He knew the trackway; it was reckoned, he said, the limit to the hunting ground in that direction.

"We've come far enough," he said, and made to turn back.

But Stephen spotted a movement just across the trackway, in what appeared to be a thicket.

"Likely the pigs have their den in there," he said, and then, "It's another old building!"

It was. The thicket, mostly sycamore and ash, had sprung up among the broken and tumbled walls of what must once have been a house standing almost alongside the trackway. Without waiting for Grandfather Tony's consent, Stephen moved stealthily across the open trackway and slid behind a thick tangle of nettles and bramble. From there he peered into the jumble of broken walls, trees and bushes. Then he beckoned us to follow.

Grandfather Tony could not ignore such an opportunity. He whispered instructions to us to surround the place, to station ourselves at the gaps the pigs had made so that, on his command, we would all rush in shouting. With luck one of us would encounter a pig trying to escape and, also with luck, be able to stun it or corner it long enough for us collectively to kill it.

We moved cautiously into place, keeping downwind. At Grandfather Tony's shout we attacked. But the tangled growth and the uneven, stone-strewn ground hampered us more than the pigs—except for Stephen. A shout from him told us he had cornered one, and John and I scrambled to him and helped him to beat the creature senseless.

Panting, we paused for Grandfather Tony to finish it off with his knife, but instead of coming forward, he stood a few paces back, his face pinched with pain and anger, and lifting one leg. He had, it seemed, caught his foot on an unevenness of the ground, and had wrenched or perhaps broken his ankle.

Stephen killed the pig with Grandfather Tony's knife. But how were the three of us to get it and Grandfather Tony back to the village? Clearly Grandfather Tony could not walk the uphill way, and for us to attempt to carry him would have meant leaving the pig, our first pig, to the wild dogs.

Grandfather Tony had to decide. After some uncertainty he said that Stephen would have to stay with him and the pig, while John and I went quickly back to the village to fetch help.

"And hurry," Grandfather Tony added, and forgetting in his pain and anxiety his earlier fears, "Go back along that trackway. It'll be quicker. Follow it until it bends away to the left, then strike straight up the Mountain."

John and I hurried off, aware of the importance of fetching help. The trackway made easier going than scrambling up through the forest. It led curving only slightly along the more level ground below the trees clambering up the slope. We knew that within an hour we would at least have reached the rim of our valley, and so would be able to whistle to whichever Grandfather was acting shepherd to pass on the news.

Just at the bend where the trackway turned from the Mountain, where Grandfather Tony meant we should strike up through the forest, we saw a sight which made both of us check our strides. To one side of the track, near where we would have to leave it, were two men. They were sitting on a fallen tree trunk, eating. Nearby were two horses—I knew them to be horses though the two that we had once owned had been killed for food in the bad winter before I left the Parents' House.

The men looked up at our approach, appearing less surprised at the sight of us than I felt at the sight of them. We had heard that other hunters used the forest and occasionally some of the Fathers had spoken with them. I had assumed that those hunters would look much like our men. But these two strangers, watching our uncertain approach with casual curiosity, looked very different. They had no beards, and their smooth faces had not the reddishness that comes from working in wind and sun. Under their dark hair, darker than any of ours, their faces looked pale—not the patchy paleness of sickness, but a kind of even paleness that hinted that they did not spend much of their time outdoors. And, as we drew nearer, I saw that the cloth of their tunics had a smoother look to it than that the Grandmothers wove.

We approached warily—at least I did. John's easy-going nature made him less suspicious. I tightened my grip on my hunting club as one of the men stood up, giving us a friendly smile.

"Hallo," he called. "Do you live around here?" He spoke in a slightly singsong way, somehow in keeping with his smile.

John said, "Over the Mountain."

"Over the mountain, eh?" asked the man. "What do you do there? Farming?"

It seemed a strange question.

The man thrust a hand into his tunic and pulled something out.

"Ever see any of this stuff about there?" he asked, taking a step towards us. He was holding out a piece of black, shining stone. "Have you ever seen any?" he repeated.

John looked at the stone with interest. I said, "No!" I wanted to be away from them, and there was Grandfather Tony waiting for help.

But John asked the man, "What is it?"

"Coal," he said. "You get it out of the ground. You can burn it—and other things. You can make machines go with it."

"Machines?" asked John, for we had never heard the word.

I said to him, "Come on, John. Grandfather's waiting—"

The man and his black stone still held John's curiosity.

"Machines that go along roads like this one," said the

man, and he tapped the dark trackway with his foot. "Machines that can carry you about."

John did not understand. The man looked at me. "You're sure you've never seen any coal like this?" he asked.

But I scarcely heard him. The phrase he had used to John—"machines that can carry you"—had caught me. It hinted of a carz, and at once I was reminded of what Susan had told me. I felt almost alarmed, but not with the recollection of her going into the Forbidden Area. It was more the feeling I had had when last I had taken up Old Carz' stores, the awareness of danger lurking beyond my little knowledge, lurking in the unknown that stretched out beyond our valley.

And we were outside the valley now, and talking with strangers. I said, "No, I haven't!" to the man and turned to go. As John did not at once follow, I called, "Come on! There's Grandfather Tony!"

John came then and we clambered up through the forest to where the trees thinned below the rise to the Mountain's ridge. I hurried; I did not want John to question me, to ask why I had so suddenly left the strangers. But as we came to the steeper slope, he caught me up.

"What did he mean?" he asked, puffing.

"I—I don't know." And then quickly, hoping to turn his thoughts away from the two pale men, "Perhaps he was having a joke."

For once John's round face did not smile at the suggestion of something to laugh about.

"I didn't think he was having a joke," he said in an

unfamiliar, serious tone. "And what did he mean when he said the black stone could carry you?"

For a moment I thought to tell John what I had read into the man's words, but he was too young and I feared that, if he realized that I thought a carz could be a reality, he might blab my credulity all over the village.

"I don't know," I said. And just then I caught sight of Grandfather Kenneth standing up by the shepherd's hut. I blew a long blast on my whistle and as he turned to see who was needing help, "Come on!" I said to John. "We must get up quickly. It'll take the Grandfathers some time to get to Grandfather Tony."

Long before we had reached the hut, Grandfather Kenneth had whistled on the message and, as John and I came over the ridge, we saw Grandfather Peter and Father Harold coming up the valley and, further down by the Houses, the little cluster of Grandmothers and Mothers watching anxiously.

We shouted to Grandfather Kenneth that Grandfather Tony had been hurt, and he began down the upper pasture towards the Headman and Father Harold. As we watched them I wondered what the Grandfathers would say if we told them about meeting the strangers. The Headman would, I guessed, be angry that we had spoken with them. Had John not been with me, I think I would have decided to say nothing, particularly as the stranger's phrase kept returning to my mind and making me uneasy. I wondered if I could persuade John not to tell but that, I knew, would make him the more curious.

The three men met near the Wall, and seemed for a

minute or two unsure what to do. Once Father Harold
turned as if to go back, probably thinking to fetch our
handcart, but no doubt Grandfather Peter realized that
to drag it down into the forest would be a slow and cum-
bersome business. At last the three of them came up
towards us.

All the time I was wondering what to say, how much
to tell. For I felt a sudden need to know what it was that
Susan had seen near the Forbidden Area. The stranger's
words had hinted that there could be such a thing as a
carz, and if that were so, I might be on the edge of finding fragments of truth in others of Old Carz' improbable
tales. . . .

At last Grandfather Peter strode up. He asked me
tersely where Grandfather Tony was. "Take us there,"
he commanded, and with Father Harold we began down
into the forest.

Before we had gone a dozen paces, John said to Grandfather Peter, "We saw two men. They had smooth faces
and—"

"What men?" asked the Headman sharply. "Strangers?"

"Yes, and they had a black—"

Grandfather Peter asked, "Did they see Tony? Were
they near him?"

"No," I replied. "And I think they were following a
kind of trackway."

Grandfather Peter nodded and strode on.

Trotting to keep up with him, John began, "They had
a funny stone. They said—"

"They must have been pedlars," said Grandfather Peter shortly.

John looked disappointed at the Headman's abrupt dismissal of what had been to him an adventure of strange significance.

There was no sign of the two pale strangers as we reached the trackway and turned towards where Grandfather Tony and Stephen were waiting. I think the strangers cannot have passed them for neither mentioned having seen them. And in the business of the next hour, John seemed to forget the men, too. We had to cut poles and gather ivy strands to make a rough stretcher for Grandfather Tony; John and I had the task of tying the pig to a pole so that we could carry it, dangling between us. Stephen took his turn with the Headman and Father Harold at carrying Grandfather Tony. The sun was low over the forest behind us as we toiled over the Mountain to reach the upper pasture. But all the way I kept thinking on the two pale strangers, and what I should say if the Headman remembered what John had said and questioned me. I decided to borrow John's puzzlement.

It was full dark by the time Stephen and John and I reached the House. We ate our belated meal by the fire's glow for in the Children's House we were not allowed rushlights and, indeed, there were seldom enough to last the Parents and the Grandparents through the winter. Stephen told of our killing the pig, heavily proud that he had first found the trail and had later been first to strike. Carole was impressed.

As Stephen paused, John said, "We saw two men. They

had smooth faces, and horses like Smith's—"

"We once had horses," I interrupted, trying to stop him.

"Did we?" asked John.

For the moment I hoped I had turned his thoughts away from the incident.

Stephen confirmed that we had had horses. "We had to kill them in the bad winter," he added. He seemed uninterested in the strangers.

But the strangers were still on John's mind. "They had a black stone," he went on. "They said it could carry people."

"Carry people?" Carole repeated, puzzled. "How big was it."

"It was quite small," John told her. "The man pulled it out of his pocket."

Stephen said, in a heavy voice that reminded me of Father Dennis, "Carry people on a bit of black stone! They must have been daft."

I said, "Grandfather Peter said they were pedlars."

"They hadn't any thin cloth," said John in a puzzled voice, for the only pedlars that came to the valley, besides the one who brought the autumn salt, carried strangely thin, bright cloth that made the Mothers' eyes open wide in wonder though they knew, of course, that it would have been useless for wearing.

John added, with a glance at me as if hoping for confirmation, "They said the black stone would burn."

None of us had ever heard of a stone that would burn.

Stephen said, "They must have been hoping you'd give them something for it. They must have been seeing if you were as daft as they were."

John looked at him in surprise. No doubt he was wondering what the men could have expected us to give them in exchange for their black stone. Clearly we had been far from our village, even if we had wanted the stone we had nothing to give for it and, being only children, we could not have exchanged a side of lamb or a sack of oats such as the Headman gave in payment to Smith.

John said no more, and soon his puckered forehead cleared of its puzzlement. But I was aware that he had truly told only part of the stranger's tale; he had said nothing about the burning of the black stone somehow driving a . . . what was the word the man had used? A— a "machine," by which I had thought he had meant a carz. I did not remind John of what he appeared to have forgotten, but as I glanced towards Susan she met my look with a questioning lift to her eyebrows and a slight smile. She must have guessed enough to know that, at the first chance we could get, I would be asking her to show me what she believed to have been a carz . . . even though we would be risking going near to the Forbidden Area.

Susan's Discovery

SUSAN AND I WENT SOONER than I expected. I thought that several days might have to pass, a week or two perhaps, before I found an opportunity to ask her out of the others' hearing. But, in fact, we went the next day but one.

It was a gray day with wisps of mist lingering down the valley and among the trees of the Waste. Since Grandfather Tony was injured, we boys could not go hunting. We had to find ourselves tasks about the House, and I had taken up a food bowl that I had shaped out of a fragment of wood left over from when Father Alan had renewed a post to the yard-gate. The bowl was nearly finished; it now needed its roughness to be smoothed with sand.

Good smoothing sand was only to be found on the edge of the Waste where the brook spread into a patch of marsh before finding its way through the mounds and tangles that blocked the lower end of the valley. I might well have to hunt a while for the sand and that would mean my searching the far side where the marsh fringed on the Waste nearer the Forbidden Area. I glanced at Carole and Stephen while I wondered if I dared risk going. The mistiness would make me indistinct to any eyes that chanced to look that way, but how to get Susan to come?

She was teaching Angela to plait rushes. To be sure, it was late to cut more but I risked saying to her, "You'll be wanting some more rushes, won't you?"

As I spoke I went over and picked up a bucket for the sand. Susan understood. She said easily, "I'd better get some more," and with a smile to Angela she added, "You're learning too quickly. I'll not be long."

Carole and Stephen, sitting beside the fire, did not even look at us as we left, though I caught a glance from John.

We waited until we were near on halfway to the Waste before speaking.

"We'll have to be quick," Susan said.

I began, "If it's in the Forbidden Area . . ."

"I don't think it's as far," Susan said. "It's in a kind of clearing with black flat stone about it. That couldn't be the Forbidden Area, could it?"

It certainly did not sound strange enough to fit my imagined picture of the place. "A clearing with black stones?" I asked, recalling the strangers John and I had spoken with.

"Not stones," Susan said. "A kind of slab of blackish stuff."

We were nearing the marsh and a short way off was that odd stretch that was like the trackway I had seen in the forest, just the few paces of it before it was lost in the Waste. "It's like that," said Susan, nodding towards the fragment of trackway.

I suddenly realized that our brief stretch of dark trackway—so familiar that I had scarcely noticed it—could have been the beginning of a long stretch like that I had seen cutting through the forest below the Mountain. Our short length could have somehow become covered by the humps and tangles of the Waste; indeed Susan's words hinted that it had been, that what she had taken to be a carz was on the continuation of our trackway. And at once the pale stranger's words came back to me, "Machines that go along roads like this one."

I asked Susan, "Could we get our cart along it?"

"Yes," she said. "Why?"

I told her about the "machines" that the stranger had mentioned to John and me. "He said it went along a—a 'road' he called it," I said. "We were on one—like the track over there but much longer. It seemed to go on and on. Could what you saw be a 'road?' "

It sounded like one but, as far as Susan could remember, it disappeared among the trees after a short way. "I don't think it went far," she added. "And these—what did you call them?"

" 'Machines.' "

"Could that mean a kind of carz?"

"It sounded like it," I agreed, "but how could the black stone have made it move?"

We were reaching the marsh. I would have gone on, but, almost as if she had thought out everything, Susan said, "You'd better get the sand first," and went quickly to cut a handful of rushes.

As I hurriedly scooped up some sand—not good smoothing sand, but it would do—I looked quickly back towards the Houses. They were blurred by the mist, but already it was thinning.

"We'll have to be quick," said Susan, and dropping the bucket I followed her into the Waste.

The brambles did not hinder us at first; we were following the paths we had used when gathering nuts and berries. Susan went so determinedly that I had to hurry to keep pace with her until she reached a bank thick with untrodden growth, mostly of hawthorn and blackthorn. It marked the farthest point that any of us had ever reached, and beyond it I could make out that the brook had carved a deep gully between the hummocks of earth. Beyond was the Forbidden Area.

Susan did not stop. She suddenly crouched down and began forcing her way under the lower branches of the thorns. "We're nearly there," she said.

The thorns caught at my back, but it was an easier way of getting through than pushing against the prickly branches. And the tilt of the ground, falling sharply, helped us.

The slope ended at the brook. Beyond it, up the far side of the gully, stretched more woodland similar to the familiar Waste though not so dense. As I caught up, I wondered how Susan had known the way. Had she dared to slip down here while fruit gathering?

"It's over there," she said with a nod towards where, I could just see, the end of the Mountain tilted towards the Waste.

I said, "That is the Forbidden Area. It must be."

"It's not so far," she said with a hint of impatience in her voice. "Look! That clearing!"

Above the far side of the gully the misty light showed a gap in the trees. Susan splashed across the brook and clambered up the opposite bank to make for it. Following, I felt my feet catching on hard unevennesses under the growth. The weeds and brambles, and the trees, too, seemed to spring out of humpy earth unlike that of our fields. But I had no time to snatch at the significance of that before we were out of the tangle and standing on a more level slab of rock smeared with the black material I had seen on the trackway through the forest. And before us, half-hidden by a hawthorn that had sprung up through a break in the slab, stood what had once been a building.

At first glance it looked less ruined than those we had seen when hunting, and I regarded it warily. Such a place might be used by wild dogs as a lair or even by men lurking in the forest. To one side, the black-covered trackway led round a clump of hollies to disappear under a fallen tree. Beyond the ruin rose up what looked like the skeleton of a building, fashioned from rusted iron, which gave the place a sinister appearance. I felt sure that, whatever Susan might believe, we were looking if not at the actual Forbidden Area, at least at a place of similar ill-omen.

Nothing stirred in the building, and Susan began to walk nearer. I followed and saw that the place was little more than a single wall. Long ago a second wall had stood perhaps half-a-dozen paces from the fairly complete one we had first seen, but had crumbled to become smothered in growth. But the roof which had joined the two walls had not fallen to the ground before decaying; it had become lodged on something within the building, something that had caught the roof and held it a few feet above the ground—

"There!" said Susan, pointing; and I saw what still held up the rotten fragments of old roof. It appeared to have been a large iron box, large enough to hold three or four people. Much of it had rusted away, but enough remained to show the shape. To one end, the end towards us, it seemed to have had a projection ending in a small opening with traces of metal bars across it, and on each side, unmistakably, were the remains of wheels.

Susan said, "Look, there are no shafts for a horse, nothing to harness to."

We had edged nearer. Being taller than Susan, I could see over the remains of the projecting front. There were two roughly rounded pieces of some strange, leatherlike material and behind them a larger piece of the same stuff.

Dead leaves and pieces of twig and branch all but filled the space between them, but they had a look like the padded mattresses the Grandparents had on their beds; if they had been flat I would have thought them for sitting on, for two people to sit in front and two more behind. In front of one of them was another wheel propped up somehow at an angle, and rising up were traces of what might have been metal walls.

It did not altogether fit my imagined picture of what Old Carz had spoken of. The projection in front was so rusted and decayed that I could not guess what its purpose had been and I had visualized no more than the box part on wheels. But the shapes inside suggesting some arrangement for four people to stand or sit, and the fact that most of it was of metal—and of a stranger shape than the iron fragments of buildings I had seen—and the clear remains of wheels, told me that it must have been what the old man meant by a carz.

Susan asked, "If it isn't a carz, what is it?"

The sight both fascinated and repelled me. It seemed to embody the mental struggle I had had when last I had been up to the old man's hut, the urge to know more, the fear of where knowing might lead. But looking at the carz, I knew that I had to go on. It told too clearly that at least sometimes Old Carz' stories were based on reality. My mind jumped—perhaps guided by the recollection of toiling up to the old man's hut—to his notion that the Wall had once stretched right across the valley, holding back the water of the brook into a huge pond, and, though the reason for such an improbable work still escaped me, I suddenly realized that the humps of the Waste over which we had just clambered could have been the result of water from such a pond suddenly released and rushing down the valley.

I told Susan of my thoughts. For a moment she could not understand why the sight of the carz had set me thinking about the Wall. But after a moment she said, "Then he is right about that too. He may be right about all sorts of things!"

"Yes, he might be!" I agreed, but again I felt that twinge of my struggle. Old Carz had told of so many strange things, I could not at once accept all of them. I said, "But why would they have wished to build the Wall to hold back the water?"

"Why did they want a carz?" asked Susan. "You'll have to ask him." And then, practical as ever, she added, "We'd better be getting back before we're missed."

We scrambled back the way we had come. It seemed to take longer than it had to go, and on the way I found something which was later to appear significant. It was a piece of thin paper, so thin that I could see through it, and some colored marks on it caught my eye. We had found such pieces before, had turned them up when digging or seen one brought down by the brook, and had taken little notice of them, but this one seemed unusual because, even as I saw it, I recognized the red and blue marks on it as Writing like that I had seen in the Headman's room.

"What is it?" asked Susan over her shoulder as I snatched it up. She was already a few paces ahead of me, hurrying back.

I didn't know if I ought to tell her that it was Writing. I could not read it, of course, but the Headman had stressed the secrecy which surrounded the skill.

"It's nothing," I said shortly, avoiding her surprised look as I slipped the paper under my tunic. "Come on, or we'll be missed."

By the time we at last reached the familiar fringe of the Waste, we seemed to have been away so long that I felt certain our absence would have been noticed. I expected to see two or three of the Fathers coming to look for us. But my bucket of sand still stood where I had left it and across the rising fields the Houses, now blurred by only the slightest hint of mist, looked indifferent to our reappearance. No one was standing at the yard-gate, no one was looking towards us.

"With luck we'll not have been noticed," Susan panted.

As we walked on up towards the Houses feeling unnaturally conspicuous, I asked her, "How did you know it was there? The carz, I mean?"

Susan replied almost casually, "Oh, I saw it one day when Carole sent me down to see if the nuts were ripe enough to pick."

"But that must have been weeks ago!" I exclaimed.

"Yes, it must have been," she replied and, as I looked my amazement that she could have kept such a secret for so long, she gave a little smile.

"Don't you ever want to know?" she asked. "I mean, we never see anyone and there's people living beyond the Mountain and below the Waste. It's almost as if they don't want us to know."

Her words echoed Old Carz: "You're kept from knowing." I had already decided that, when next I took up his stores, I would ask him more. I felt a sudden need to know, to understand. I would tell him about the carz, of course, and he would be able to read the fragment of writing, too, and beyond those were other hints of realities that I wanted to know about.

"Old Carz!" I said. "He'll be able to tell—"

Suddenly I stopped.

"What's the matter?" asked Susan, with a quick look towards the Houses. "Keep walking or someone may notice."

"It's the Reading and Writing," I whispered with sudden alarm. "Old Carz is hoping I'll be chosen. He's told me he's writing down—something, I'm not sure what. All he can remember, I suppose. But I may not be chosen—"

"You must be," she said. "John's too young and Stephen —he'd never learn."

"But I annoyed Grandfather Peter!"

"How?"

"I—it was something I knew about what he showed us," I began, but I could say no more. It would have meant telling her about what had happened in the Headman's room, and that was secret. "I—I can't tell you," I said.

Susan looked at me almost sharply. At the time I thought she was annoyed that I had, by angering Grandfather Peter, made it unlikely that I would ever learn to read what Old Carz had written, but later I found myself wondering if her look, steady, with no trace of a smile in it, told that she suspected that the secrecy which wrapped the Headman's doings was part of the means by which we were, as she said, "kept from knowing."

We were too near the Houses to say more. As we entered the yard, my new uncertainty was such that I almost expected someone to come out, to demand where we had been and why. But we saw only Grandmother Mary and she, as ever, gave us a full-cheeked smile.

We went on into the Children's House, but Carole was not there to demand why we had taken so long to fetch a little sand and a few rushes. Nor was Stephen there. It seemed he had been persuaded to accompany Carole up to Old Carz' hut with his stores. Little Angela, busily instructing Patrick in the mysteries of plaiting rushes, was delighted with Susan's handful. Only John looked at us, and that to grin.

"First it's Carole and Stephen," he said. "Now it's you two. I'll soon be oldest boy! . . . And you've torn your tunic," he added to me.

Susan answered for me with a naturalness that seemed almost unnatural. "I noticed that when you came back from the hunting," she said. "I'll mend it before I forget again."

And that was all. When, a few minutes later, Carole

and Stephen came in, they scarcely glanced at us. It seemed incredible to me that no one had noticed our going and, almost as incredible, that no one knew of our momentous discovery. And without anyone seeing I was able to hide that fragment of thin, lettered paper under my mattress.

But I was troubled a little that Carole, no doubt for the excuse it gave her and Stephen to be on their own, had resumed taking up Old Carz' stores. I was wanting to see the old man, to ask him about the writing I had found, to tell him that Susan and I had seen a carz. I would then see the keenness light his old eyes, the hope that at last someone knew that what he told was not all makebelieve. I hoped that next time I would be able to go up with his stores.

I did not know then that there was to be no next time.

The Reading
and the Writing

THE MISTINESS that had helped Susan and me to venture, unobserved, near to the Forbidden Area and so discover the carz, foretold a change in the weather. The next night the wind sprang up, and from the north; the next afternoon the snow began.

It came not gently as often in previous winters but with a sudden fury, driving clouds of snowflakes before it, piling them around the Houses, rushing inside whenever we risked opening a door. We knew again why the three Houses of the village had been built to form with the big barn a square, its stout windowless walls outwards. The wind howled around it, the snow smote against it, but the buildings stood firm against the onslaught. Our village had been built to protect us from such fury as well as from strangers or the wild dogs of the forest whom we heard in the nights howling above the whine of the wind.

And when after four long, bitter days the storm eased, the cold remained. Stephen and I helped the Fathers clearing the snow from the yard, but beyond the gate we could see a white world. All the familiar tilts and hollows had been smoothed by the snow and down towards the Waste a great drift hid even the field walls, while another drift seemed almost to close in the valley up by the Wall.

John did not help in the snow clearing. Though sturdily made, he was inclined to take chills during the winter, and the second night of the storm he had lain coughing in his bunk. In the morning Carole had sent for Mother Rachel who usually acted nurse, and John had been taken over to the Parents' House where a corner was fitted out with bed, bowls and such medicaments as we had. I wondered, as he went, whether he would recover soon enough to be chosen by the Headman as next Learner; for I knew it was likely that Grandfather Peter would occupy some of the time the snow kept us indoors with teaching whomever he chose.

Grandfather Peter sent for me. I think now that had the snow lasted but a few days he would have delayed his decision, but as the chill winds persisted and as it became likely a week or more before any outdoor work could be done, the opportunity to spend at least some of the time on the teaching could not be missed. It was several years since anyone had been chosen and then it had been Charles who had died of a sickness within a year or two. The need to find a replacement and so keep at least one in each generation knowledgeable in the skills had become a necessity. I think, too, that had Stephen been a year or two younger and had he shown some little aptitude, he would have taken preference over me. As it was, with John still sick, the Headman truly had no choice.

Grandfather Peter was far from welcoming. Though I felt a tingling of pride as I walked to his room under the watching eyes and approving smiles of the Grandparents, my pride abruptly fled as I opened the door. To me the Headman was still a figure of awe, and as I came face to face with him, something near to fear gripped me. His tall, hunch-shouldered body seemed almost to fill the little room. He towered over me and his slight stoop thrust his face close to mine; I could see the faint veins on his jutting nose and my own reflection in the little sunken eyes that seemed to be piercing my thoughts. I was suddenly afraid that somehow he had come to know that Old Carz had told me of his writings, or that he had heard about our discovery of the carz, and it was for this that he had sent for me. I felt a sense of relief when, after a long stare, he told me to sit down on the stool facing him across the little table.

After another pause he told me curtly that I had been chosen. In my fear I was ready to assume a reluctance in his manner which did not diminish as he added, almost as an excuse, "The snow looks like lasting a while yet." But, once started on the teaching, he seemed himself more at ease. He began by repeating much of what he had said to John and Stephen and me about the need for secrecy, adding as he turned to take two of the boards from the shelf, "You had better forget that old document I showed you. It will be a long time before you need to know about such things." And unexpectedly he smiled as if he was trying to reassure me, but his little eyes, deep in their sockets, still remained sharp and watchful.

"And now to work," he said, holding out a Rule board to me.

His method of teaching was simple and crude. He read a line of word-shapes, I repeated it. As soon as I had one line right, he went on to the next until after perhaps a half-hour we had reached the last line. He worked with a kind of deliberate persistence, almost as if the words meant little to him; or it may have been that he was unaccustomed to the teaching and could not foresee my possible difficulties. Though I managed to pick out a word-shape here and there, he did not draw my attention to any similarities in the shapes before my still-uneasy gaze; nor did his phrasing give any meaning to the words. I just repeated the Rules line by line with scarcely any awareness of what I was saying.

When we reached the last line, he went back to the beginning, and again we went through the whole board. I suppose I must have had a fairly retentive memory for I followed him quite well, but I was uneasy that I was not grasping any meaning in the words. Perhaps he glimpsed something of my uncertainty for once, as I stumbled, he said something about my coming to understand the Rules when I was older, and again I caught his smile, the lips twisting without bringing a corresponding lightening into his little eyes.

So we must have progressed for perhaps an hour when there was a tentative tap at the door. Grandfather Peter lifted his long body from his stool and, with a look of annoyance on his face, went to open the door. I heard Grandmother Mary's anxious, whispered apology and then the Headman said irritably, "I have said so." As if Grandmother Mary was still dissatisfied, he added, "All right, I'll come!" and went out.

Left alone I felt relieved. For a full hour I had experienced the unease of his presence, and for much of that time I had wanted to break off from the endless repetition to see if I could make out at least a few of the word-shapes. As his absence lengthened into minutes I took to looking at the lines of word-shapes and, by repeating to myself the first line or two and at the same time looking along the line, I managed to pick out a few shapes whose meaning I could guess; and then, feeling I had made something of a discovery, I began searching through other lines for more of the same shapes. I had even been able to build two or three adjoining shapes into a phrase or two that I remembered, though I was, as yet, quite unaware of the idea of individual letters having their own sounds.

It was not until I heard Grandfather Peter coming back

that I recalled the strange board, the one with the gray picture of the men chasing the round object and the list of battles of the Old Days; and I realized that if I had dared to search for it, the Headman's absence would have given me the opportunity. As it was, he returned to tell me to go. Perhaps my disappointment showed on my face —for I had felt on the point of discovering the significance of the word-shapes—for he said, not unkindly, "We'll try again tomorrow." He added, with that disturbing smile of his, "Too much at one go wouldn't be good for you."

I left the room to walk between the beds of the Grandparents to the House door. The Headman's last words had revived my feeling of pride. But, this time, I was not greeted with approving smiles, except from Grandmother Mary whose face seemed not to have its usual warm fullness. The other Grandparents appeared wrapped in thought and Grandfather Tony, his leg still bandaged, stared into the fire, his wizened face more anxiously lined than ever.

I was so full of my achievement, and perhaps disappointed that they paid so little heed of me—for to be chosen was still a matter of pride—that their restrained appearance did not impress itself on me at the time. It was not until later that I suddenly realized what they must all have been thinking about, what must have prompted Grandmother Mary's visit to the Headman's room. By then I had had another hour with Grandfather Peter and before the lesson ended had been able to say, prompted only by the word-shapes I had come to recognize, several phrases unaided. Grandfather Peter had appeared impressed—for, as I was to learn later, his other pupil, Father Dennis, had relied more on memory than on the skill of reading to tell the Rules. As I crossed the yard back to the Children's House afterwards, I felt again a thrill of achievement so that I scarcely noticed Father Dennis and Father Alan looking out over the snowy landscape from the yard-gate until Father Alan's voice caught my ear.

"We could supply him for another week or two," he was saying, his tone persuasive. "The weather may break enough to let us go hunting. . . ."

Father Dennis's heavy voice had interrupted him. "It's the Rule," he said. "And we'll have little enough to get us through the winter as it is."

My feeling of pride suddenly fled as I guessed whom they were talking about and recalled Grandmother Mary's visit to the Headman. I did not have to go to the yard-gate and look up the valley towards the hut by the Wall for confirmation of my sudden fear. There would, I knew, be no footprints in the snow leading up there. Old Carz had, as we said, "been left."

I remember I went in and sat on my bunk without noticing what the others were doing. I felt alone in a way I had never felt before. As I sat there Susan glanced at me, her eyebrows slightly lifted in question, but that somehow only increased my feeling of apartness. I did not know whether or not I was allowed to tell her what I had overheard of the Fathers' talk. That feeling of restraint, the awareness that we were wrapped around in ignorance, suddenly seemed stronger than ever before—and not only because of the shock of realizing that I might never be able to tell the old man of our discovery of the carz. It was as if the restraints under which we lived had come right into our separate lives. Not only did we know so little of what went on beyond our valley; we were as individuals being kept apart, as if beyond the day-to-day business of living we were to have no more contact with one another's ideas and hopes and thoughts than as a community we were permitted with the outside world. I could not even openly share with Susan the news that the old man had "been left."

As I sat there feeling this greater restriction, Old Carz up in his hut seemed to personify our individual apartness, for in truth he was separated from us by the ways of our thinking and living far more than by the distance and the snow. It was not merely the fact that he had "been left" that troubled me though, recalling the look in his eyes on my last visit, that added a wrench of sorrow. The "leaving" was, we had all come to realize, a necessity for most winters the twenty or so of us had struggle enough to eke out our food and to keep ourselves and our stock without having to support those who, through old age or sickness, could no longer work; indeed the Founder, when framing the Rule, had probably assumed that, as then the oldest, he would be the first of the village to "be left." But now I was coming to see that there could be more in the leaving of Old Carz than necessity and the Rule. For as long as I could remember he had lived apart from the rest of us—and I began to suspect that it was not only his crippled foot and the limitations that had put on his work which had prompted the separation. His strange stories— for those who might come to accept some of them—could unsettle the kind of life that had been imposed on us. Our mockery and disbelief had been allowed—or encouraged? —to create a barrier between us and his knowledge. It was almost as if someone—Grandfather Peter? Father Dennis? —had been waiting for such a winter as this to put an end to the old man's disturbing tales.

And on a nearer, more personal level there was the memory of my last visit to the hut, of the hopefulness that I had seen in his look when he had thought I had been chosen to learn the Reading and Writing. I wished sud- denly that I could go to him, could tell him of my choos- ing, could tell him, too, of Susan's discovery, of how we— she and I—were coming to find realities in what we had all for so long jeered at as fantasies. And I wished, too, that I could have assured him that something of his knowl- edge would not die with him. But I dared not go, I dared not risk leaving a trail in the snow for all to see.

I can recall little of the rest of that day. It must have been well into the afternoon that, being near Susan when the others were occupied, I risked whispering to her that Old Carz had "been left." She gave a long, slightly winc- ing look—though whether from pity for the old man or from the realization that our one contact with the knowl- edge of the Old Days was being broken, I could not tell. But later, as we prepared ourselves for the night, she asked quietly, "His writings? Will anyone find them?" And then, without waiting for my answer, she added, "Carole has not said she's seen them. She would have. Could he have hidden them somewhere?"

She could say no more then for Carole was coming our way. But afterwards, as I lay on my bunk, I wondered what the old man would do with his writings. It was not likely that he would just leave them for anyone to find—though when I had seen him at the writing he had made no attempt to conceal it.

I found myself again thinking back over that last time I had gone up to the hut. Again in my mind I saw the hopefulness lighting his shadowed eyes, again I heard the unexpected keenness in his voice as he had spoken of the time when I would come to read his writings; and then I saw myself hurrying away from him, running back from the fringe of the unknown to the known, scrambling over the blocks of stone as if—

My mind lurched. Those rocks had recalled Old Carz' tale of their once being part of the Wall which had, in the phrase he persisted in using, "been blown up" . . . and my thoughts flashed back to the Headman showing John and Stephen and me that old document with its strange picture of the men running near a round object, a "bomb" Grandfather Peter had called it, and he had said something about its being dangerous, killing people, destroying buildings. Could that have been what Old Carz had meant? Could a "bomb," whatever that was, have destroyed the middle of the Wall?

I let the possibility sink into my mind. It was another

matter I would have asked the old man about, another hint of the reality that we had been led to disbelieve.

The feeling of restraint, of being kept from knowing, took on a sharper and more sinister definition when, next morning, I went over to the Headman's room for my lesson. Grandfather Peter was not waiting for me, but Father Dennis instead. It was, I now realize, natural enough that the only other man skilled in the Reading should take a turn at teaching the Rules to make sure that he had not himself forgotten them, but at the time Father Dennis's surly greeting sounded almost threatening. He it was who had told Father Alan that Old Carz must "be left." Though the Headman must have given the order, could Father Dennis have persuaded him to do so? Had he now come to hear me in order to report to the Headman that I was unsuited to continue as Learner? Had he—or perhaps Grandfather Peter himself—learnt of Old Carz' writings and was seeking an excuse to dismiss me and so make sure I never gained the skill to read them?

Perhaps such fears helped me, and made me determined to show what I had so far learned. I remember that before the lesson had gone far I had gained confidence from Father Dennis's shortcomings as teacher. A bulky, slow-moving, slow-speaking man, he soon showed me that he remembered less of his learning than I had already acquired.

He told me to read, and I began with Rule One easily enough. But at Rule Four I stumbled. " 'All work is to be shared . . .' " but the next word halted me.

With what sounded like a hint of triumph, Father Dennis prompted, " '. . . except for men who are injured or sick . . .' "

I did not immediately repeat the words as I would have done with Grandfather Peter. I knew the shape of "people" came early in that Rule. Father Dennis lifted his head, but his look, dull-eyed and sullen, did not chill me as Grandfather Peter's piercing eyes would have done.

Probably with a trace of pertness, I read. " '. . . except for *people* who are injured or sick . . .' "

As I read on to the end of the Rule, I was aware that Father Dennis was looking at me and not at the board. When I had finished he scratched his beard as if annoyed, and grunted, "Go to Rule Fourteen."

With the Headman I had, so far, worked my way through the Rules from the first to the last. I suspected that, by varying the order, Father Dennis was trying to trap me. But I got through Rule Fourteen easily enough, and when he demanded Rule Thirteen I managed that also with only a stumble or two.

"Rule Twelve," he said sullenly.

I tried, but the words did not come easily. The Rule, I knew, dealt with Smith's visits, but after the word "Smith" came a little sequence of small word-shapes that were still confusing to me.

Again with triumph in his voice, Father Dennis began, " 'The smith is not to go into the houses . . .' "

Again I knew he had made a slip. There was no likelihood that Smith, when he called to do our repairs, would take his brazier and anvil into one of the Houses; he always worked well away, down by the brook. And I knew that the shape for "houses" did not appear in that Rule.

Father Dennis had given me the start. With returning confidence I began, " 'The smith is not to go into the *yard* at any time ...' "

Father Dennis's look sharpened at the word "yard." With a grunt he turned and snatched up several of the boards from the shelf. He spread three or four of them before him on the table and began studying them, his head moving ponderously from one to the next.

I watched him, hoping that he would not suddenly look up and see the delight I was feeling at having again caught him out. With a thick finger he worked his way along a line or two, his lips forming the words.

As he was so occupied, I noticed something that I had missed when reading with Grandfather Peter. On the board I was holding the words had all been written at the same time and by the same hand, but on the board Father Dennis was laboriously studying only the first eleven Rules were in the same writing. The others had been added later. I glanced at my board and saw that the Rule which was causing Father Dennis's trouble was one of the added ones. I can still remember it. THE SMITH IS NOT TO GO INTO THE YARD AT ANY TIME. HE IS TO WORK DOWN BY THE BROOK AND NO ONE EXCEPT THE GRANDPARENTS ARE TO TALK WITH HIM. Before, with the Headman, I had merely repeated the words line by line, now, suddenly, they took on a meaning, and one that brought back my suspicions that we were being deliberately confined, mentally as well as physically, within our sheltered valley. We understood—at least we children did—that we left Smith alone at his work, even though we sometimes watched from a distance the sparks fly as he sharpened a sickle or hammered a piece of iron into a new colter. It was what we had always done. But now I realized that a Rule forbade us—and the Parents, too—from speaking with Smith; and he was almost our only visitor, our only means of knowing about the world beyond our valley. To be sure, he sometimes chatted with one or other of the Grandfathers and they, in turn, passed on his news, but a Rule laid down that we should not speak with him, not question him directly about his news, not learn of the outside world from him. And that Rule was not one laid down by the Founder, it had been added by a later hand.

By then Father Dennis had found the word he was seeking. Grudgingly he told me to read another Rule and another. Each time I managed without much stumbling. At last he seemed to give up and muttered, "You're near on ready to try the Writing. We'll see what you make of that." He added, more sharply, "Take care that it doesn't turn your mind as it did Grandfather Philip's."

That last thrust was, I felt, the stroke of one defeated but wishing to gain some little point, but it turned my mind on to Grandfather Philip. And afterwards, as I sat on my bunk while the fire's glow deepened as night set in, I found myself thinking of the old story and wondering what lay behind it.

I had never known Grandfather Philip, of course; his mysterious disappearance had occurred when the Parents were children, at the time when Great-grandfather Robert had been Headman. That would have been, I reckoned, a full forty years ago, for I knew Grandfather Leonard had been Headman after Robert until he fell sick and died, when Grandfather Peter was chosen. And during those long-ago years, Old Carz must have been one of the Grandfathers, but he had not been chosen Headman even though he was the Founder's nephew and knew the Reading and Writing. Of course, it might have been that his crippled foot had prevented the choice . . . if he had been crippled for as long as that.

Suddenly I felt how little I knew even of our own past. Never had I heard how and when Old Carz had come by his injury, and the knowledge seemed now important. For if he had still been in full strength at the time when Grandfather Leonard had been chosen Headman, for what reason could he have been passed over?

I had never known any other Headman than Grandfather Peter, had never witnessed the way by which the Headman was chosen. I had assumed that there was some discussion among the Grandparents before the decision was made. Why, I kept asking, was it that other Grandfathers had been chosen in preference to the Founder's nephew and one who had lived in the village from the Foundation? Could there have been some disagreement between the Great-grandparents or the Grandparents, a split into two rival groups one of which, like Old Carz, knew of and perhaps even wished to follow the ways of the world beyond our Mountain, while the other group were fearful of the risks that such contact might hold and so had guided first the Parents and later us children into our present secluded way of living? And where in all this did the story of Grandfather Philip fit? Had he been among those who came to believe in Old Carz' notions? Had that been the basis for the others' assumption of his madness? Had that in some way led to his mysterious end?

The questions crowded in on me and again I found myself wishing desperately that I could go up for a last visit to Old Carz in his snowbound hut. Once I even looked out of the window at the thickening darkness and wondered if I dared to risk slipping out. But the snow would betray me, and once it became known that I had deliberately sought out the old man, my learning would be finished and with it any possibility of reading what he had written—if ever I should come across it.

And what chance would I have of that, I wondered. If any writings were found in the hut they would be taken by the Headman and, if not destroyed, would be kept in secret . . . unless Old Carz, realizing such a likelihood, had hidden them somewhere safe. He may well have done so and had I but listened a little longer to him, had I not run so hastily away when he had spoken of his writings, he might have given me some clue to the hiding-place.

That evening the others were almost as silent as I.

Angela and Patrick had already gone unprotesting to their bunks. Stephen and Carole, sitting on the far side of the fire, were for once not whispering together. Susan's knitting lay on her lap as she stared into the fire.

As I glanced at them, Stephen said, as if continuing a conversation the beginning of which I had missed, "It's the only way to make the food last. And, anyway he's not done any real work for years."

I guessed they had heard that Old Carz had "been left"; Carole would have been told when she had gone to ask about taking up the stores. The news, it seemed, had upset her.

She said, "It's a bit hard. He didn't eat much, and he wasn't doing anyone any harm."

"He wasn't doing any good either," said Stephen bluntly. "He could hardly walk."

"That wasn't his fault," protested Carole, her protective motherliness aroused. She added, a little unexpectedly, "And he could walk a bit when he had to."

I saw Susan glance at her, but her voice was quiet, almost incurious, as she asked, "Why do you think he could walk when he wanted to?"

"Well, the last time Stephen and me went up," Carole told her, "he was coming down from higher up the Wall. He must have gone quite a way up beside it. Don't you remember, Stephen, I said it at the time, I said I reckoned he could get about quite a bit in spite of his crippled foot."

Stephen asked, uninterestedly, "So what?"

I noticed that Susan's eyes had sharpened. She glanced at me in unspoken question, and I realized how she had interpreted Carole's words.

I realized, too, that from the door of his hut Old Carz could have seen who was coming up the valley almost as soon as they left the yard-gate. He must have seen Carole and Stephen set out up the path. But if he had gone up beside the Wall to hide his writing, surely he would have done so long before they were near enough to notice what he was doing?

Or had he assumed that they were not going to the hut but were on their way to the upper pasture? The fact that Stephen had accompanied Carole might have made him think so. And he had probably been hoping that I would bring up his stores. He might not have realized their purpose until they had left the path and were only a few minutes' scrambling distance away. That would have alarmed him; they might see his writings. And so he would have hurried to hide the writings as quickly as his crippled foot allowed.

Susan and I exchanged glances. Our thoughts had reached the same point. Somewhere along the foot of the Wall above the hut Old Carz may have made a hiding-place. It was only a possibility and one which, while the snow lasted, neither of us dared to try. But it held a trace of hope.

The Forbidden Area

FOR NEAR ON A MONTH THE SNOW STAYED, and when at last it began to melt, it did so reluctantly. A chilly dampness set in with hard frosts at night. It seemed as if winter would never go. And all that while John stayed in the Parents' House though his coughing had eased, we heard. And all that while Old Carz stayed in his hut.

I had time enough to go on to the Writing. Grandfather Peter set me to copying the Rules so that I should come to learn the word-shapes. At first, since suitably smooth board was scarce, I had to try writing in a layer of moist sand smoothed on his table, making the word-shapes laboriously with a sharpened stick. I could make only a few at a time; then I would have to wait while Grandfather Peter, or more rarely Father Dennis, checked them before smoothing them away, moistening the sand afresh, and trying me on a few more.

I progressed, I suppose, more quickly than Grandfather Peter had expected—though I was more urged by the desire to master the skill in order to be able to read Old Carz' writings than to earn the Headman's approval. Indeed, as the days passed I felt more and more uneasy in his presence—not so much a return to the fear I had had at first but, rather, a growing awareness of uncertainty within the man himself. He, for his part, seemed to be more friendly. At times he would lean back on his stool, his tight mouth twisted in a smile and, after remarking approvingly on my work, he would tell me again that I must keep the knowledge secret. Or he would suddenly lean forward, his face close to mine, and say that when I was older I would come to understand the dangers in sharing the knowledge I was now acquiring; or he might explain that "there were once some among us who forgot the disasters that such knowledge could bring to us." He hinted at times that I had been specially chosen; he talked of my "great responsibilities," of how one day I might be "among the few from whom the Headman would be chosen." When he spoke in such a way my unease deepened.

I was, I think, becoming increasingly aware that he was acting apart, that he was trying to guide me into his own ways of thinking even though he himself was not wholly sure of them. At such moments I had to turn away from him, to look down at the words I had written to avoid his eyes or, perhaps, from fear that he might glimpse my suspicions. He seemed to mistake my uneasiness for a keenness to be at work again—and so, to my relief, resumed his teaching. But growing in my mind was a mistrust of the man. The decision that Old Carz should "be left," I recalled, had been his.

Often I was left alone for several minutes at a time. I was tempted to try to find the strange board that held the "document" telling of the Old Days, but only twice did I dare to risk the Headman's anger by looking for it and then only after seeing him go over to the big barn. But the "document" was not on the shelf; I found only one crumpled fragment of paper which showed a stained picture of some men, strangely dressed in large hats and holding a long, very thick kind of rope, while behind them a towering building looked to be on fire. Underneath was what appeared to be writing, but its little letters were quite unlike those in which the Rules were written. The other "document" was no longer there. Had Grandfather Peter, I wondered, deliberately hidden it? Did he not dare to risk my finding it in case I asked questions that he did not want to answer?

Another time when Grandfather Peter was out of the room I made a discovery about the Writing—at least, it seemed a discovery to me though people who have learned the skill in the usual way would scarcely have noticed it. I remember it was the word "people" with its two p's that gave me the first clue to the idea of letters having sounds; and on a thought I hunted through what I had written and so found other letters which appeared in words having similar sounds . . . though I was several times baffled by unexpected oddities in the spelling of many words. But by the time the Headman told me I was skilled enough to make my own copy of the Rules on one of the few remaining smooth boards, I had acquired sufficient understanding of letters to risk trying such words as JERALD and SOOSAN and HEDMAN for myself while I awaited his return.

Once Grandfather Peter came back while I was so trying out my discovery, and instinctively I tried to hide my efforts. His look, suddenly suspicious, checked me from smearing the sand, and he lifted my hand to look at what I had been doing. After a long pause, his mouth smiled and he asked, in a tone lighter than usual, "Why not try, Gerald? One day perhaps you will need to add a Rule or two of your own." And he went on to suggest words for me to try—names of Parents and Grandparents mostly. But I found it difficult to write them. His remark that I might one day have to add to the Rules had reminded me of the Rule about not speaking with Smith, and instead of concentrating on what I was doing I kept wondering if it had been he who had added that restricting Rule.

It must have been later that day when I recalled the fragment of thin paper I had found as Susan and I were hurrying back from seeing the carz. I had scarcely thought of it since I had hidden it under my mattress. But perhaps my growing understanding of the Reading had brought it to mind again because now I could hope to make out its few words. When I got back to our House, I took it out unnoticed and, in the privacy of the latrine, looked at it.

There were only two words on it but, with thought of the Rule dealing with Smith's visits still in my mind, they startled me. For the first word, the one in red, said, SMITHS. I stared at it for several seconds before I tried to read the word in blue. As well as I could make it out it said, CRISPS. I did not know the word but its association with the unmistakable SMITHS made it more than puzzling. And the fact that the paper had been so near to the Forbidden Area added a disturbing possibility. As Susan and I had seen, iron skeletons of buildings stood about the place. Could Smith, I wondered, have gone there and seen the precious metal but been disturbed by the Headman and forced to leave? Was the fragment of thin paper his means of marking the spot so that he might one day steal back? and yet the man had seemed open about paying for finds of iron, and he had never, for as long as I could remember, come other than by way of the path over the Mountain. The paper and its clear association with Smith was baffling, the more so as I recalled the finding of it; it had looked as if it had lain unnoticed for years, as if Susan or I, when hurrying to the carz, had happened to disturb its covering of fallen leaves.

That strange paper was on my mind when, next morn-

ing, I went again to the Headman's room and, had I not
come to feel so unsure about him, I think I might have
told him of it. But he was as ever sharp and watchful,
though he smiled as he set before me the smooth, unused
board and told me to begin my own copy of the Rules.

I began uncertainly—at first I dipped my writing stick
so slightly in the soot-and-water paste that I could
scarcely make a mark—but after a little while I got the
trick of it. I felt proud as I saw my letters forming the first
line of Rule One, and then, under Grandfather Peter's
watchful eyes, went on to the second line.

It was a slow, painstaking business and for perhaps an
hour I worked with careful persistence—until we were interrupted by a commotion in the Grandparents' House,
a hurrying of feet as if all were making for the door, and
Father Dennis burst in to tell the Headman, "There's
pigs in the lower pasture!"

It was not unusual in the bitter weather for animals to
be driven by the wild dogs to break through from the
Waste or even over the field walls along the ridge of the
Mountain, but Father Dennis's unnaturally excited tone
surprised both of us. Grandfather Peter at once hurriedly
followed him out into the yard, and curiosity urged me
there, too. It was not until I was joining the crowd at the
yard-gate that I recalled that the diversion could have
given me another opportunity to look for that strange
"old document."

Everyone was staring over the yard-gate, everyone but
three of the Fathers who had seized their hunting clubs

and gone running into the lower pasture. The chance of adding a carcass or two of fresh pig to our stores was too welcome to miss. It seemed that a herd of pigs—seven, I counted—had suddenly broken through from the Waste; but the wild dogs that were expected to have set them on such a flight were nowhere to be seen.

Grandfather Peter demanded who had first seen the pigs. It was Susan. "I saw them come out," she said.

The Headman turned sharply to her. "You did, girl? Did you see why they came? Did you see any dogs after them?"

"No," said Susan quietly. "They just came."

He asked her if she was sure; clearly he had read something disturbing into the fact that the pigs had not been followed by chasing dogs. But Susan did not change her account. The pigs, it seemed, had just appeared rushing out of the Waste.

As the Headman turned away from her, Susan looked at me. She had guessed, as others were coming to guess, that if wild dogs had not disturbed the pigs, they must have been frightened by strangers. And both of us had glimpsed the Headman's unease at such a possibility.

For a few moments our attention was diverted by the sight of two of the Fathers cornering a pig in an angle of the field walls. One of them—it looked like Father Alan—struck a lucky blow, and soon they were bending over the carcass. The other pigs had escaped by turning back along the wall and so regaining the Waste.

The Headman was asking Father Dennis to go to the Waste to investigate.

"Shall I go alone?" Father Dennis asked.

Grandfather Peter hesitated, looking across to where the pigs' hoofprints had first disturbed the snow's smoothness. It was beyond the marsh, towards the Forbidden Area. Fathers Alan and Timothy, bearing their catch, had begun back towards us.

"Take Timothy with you," the Headman told Father Dennis, and he added, "You'd better not go all the way."

Again I was aware of Susan's glance. Like me she had guessed that the pigs must have been disturbed near the Forbidden Area and, no doubt, she had linked that fact with the place where the carz was hidden.

Susan asked me casually, "Could they have been looking for it?"

To anyone else her question would have meant little, but I had no doubt what was in her mind.

I tried to assume her casual tone. "I shouldn't think so. Any other hunters would have chased them into the pasture." And, under cover of the movement as the little crowd of us began to disperse, I added in a whisper, "More likely they were after the black stones."

Just for a moment she looked puzzled, and then her eyes cleared as with a nod towards John's retreating back, she asked, "You mean the ones you two were shown?"

Perhaps John had overheard something of what we were saying. He looked back at us and asked, "What do you think men could be after in the Waste? Could they have been the men we saw—"

Susan interrupted him, "You shouldn't be out in the cold, should you?"

Grandmother Mary nearby began, "I should think not with your cough not cured!" And, as she hustled John back into the Parents' House, "Why Rachel should have let you out of bed, I don't know!"

I looked round quickly to see if the Headman was near enough to have overheard; but he was still at the yard-gate. Catching my glance, he smiled thinly. "Back to work, Gerald!" he called. "You mustn't let anything interrupt your learning." I went back into his room and resumed my writing.

It must have been a half-hour later when Father Dennis returned. He came blustering into the Headman's room, blurting out, "It was strangers. We found their horses' tracks. They'd come near—"

A sharp look from Grandfather Peter checked him. In a carefully level voice, the Headman said to me, "You'd better go now, Gerald. You'll have to finish tomorrow."

I went out. As I walked along between the rows of the Grandparents' beds I caught the looks of concern on the old faces. And suddenly I came near to understanding their anxieties. It was not so much a conscious realization as a kind of sympathetic awareness that only now can I put into words. Unlike us children, and perhaps the Parents too, they had not needed guiding into ignorance of the world beyond our valley; having passed their childhoods within only a decade or two of the Upheaval, they had been nearer than we to the dangers they had missed. To them, ignorance meant not so much an absence of knowledge as a defense against dangers. The possibility

that, at last, strangers from the outside were approaching
our valley hinted of an end to the safe seclusion in which
they had lived and which they had, perhaps unwittingly,
encouraged us to accept.

But then, tingling from Father Dennis's blundering
alarm, I paid little heed to what the Grandparents might
be thinking. I wanted to tell Susan what I had overheard
and to ask her if, when we had seen the carz, she had
noticed any of the strange black stones about the place.
I felt that we were on the edge of another discovery, and
one that could lead to more understanding of what Old
Carz had for years been trying to tell us all.

As if she had been expecting my exciting news, Susan
was busying herself apart from the others, sitting on her
bunk, knitting. I ventured to whisper, "It *was* strangers
and near the Forbidden Area."

She nodded.

I went on, "Do you remember seeing any of the black
stones near—"

Her glance over my shoulder warned me and, turning,
I saw Carole looking towards us and stretching up to her
full bulk as if about to demand what we were whispering
about.

"I'll help you with the potatoes!" Susan called to her,
and dropped her knitting on to her bunk. We dared say
no more.

The news—there could be no hiding it—that strangers
had penetrated the Waste was soon to spread something
near to alarm through our valley. But for the moment it

showed that the snow had gone enough for us to get outdoors and that meant there was, as the Headman an-
nounced, "a first job to be done."

By next morning we all knew what that "first job"
was. We went out to the yard-gate to watch. Already the
Grandfathers, led by the Headman and Father Dennis,
had gone up the valley. Their trail in the thinning snow
led towards Old Carz' hut.

Grandmother Mary, her smile wavering, told me I had
better wait by the yard-gate. "You may be needed now
you know the Reading and the Writing," she said.

We all knew what was about to happen. Every one of
us was looking up towards the Wall and the hut, and
soon the Grandfathers and Father Dennis were beginning
the walk down the valley path, and the shape of the long,
blanket-wrapped burden they carried on their shoulders
was unmistakable. Old Carz was, we all knew, to be "returned to the earth."

They came slowly down the path. When they reached
the yard-gate, they paused while Grandfather Peter
opened the gate to the lower pasture. Then they went
on across it, making for the far side of the valley where
the growth of the Waste wrapped the Forbidden Area.

At the edge of the Waste they paused again. For a few
moments they seemed unsure what to do; and then, lay-
ing the body on the ground, Grandfather Brian and
Grandfather Kenneth began to walk back towards us. I
heard a whispered buzz about me, caught Grandmother
Mary's protest, "But he's so young!" and knew what was
to happen. Only those knowledgeable in the Reading and

Writing, those from whom future Headmen would be chosen, were allowed into the Forbidden Area. Among the adults the distinction was shared by only Grandfather Peter and Father Dennis. With a sickening feeling that I knew I must not show, I watched the two Grandfathers approaching.

Before they reached the yard-gate, Grandfather Brian called, "Gerald, you're to go! You'll need a sickle." He added, as if in explanation to the others, "They'll be able to manage if the way's cleared a bit."

I was aware that Father Alan thrust a sickle into my hand and gave me a pat on the shoulder. "You'll be all right, boy," he said. And then I began walking on unsteady legs down the slope to the brook. I stumbled as I reached it, and again as I began across the lower pasture towards where the Headman and Father Dennis were waiting.

Grandfather Peter said more gently than I had ever heard him speak, "You'll have to come. There's no one else." He nodded towards the first growths of the Waste. "You go ahead and cut us a way. Go only a step or two in front, and stop the moment I tell you."

Keeping my eyes averted from the blanket-wrapped shape on the ground, I went and began hacking at the first clump of dead brambles. It helped to be doing something. Quickly I cut a way through and then, as I went on, Grandfather Peter and Father Dennis followed with their burden.

Though I scarcely noticed it, there were fewer brambles than on the familiar side of the Waste. Gaps of several paces at a time were covered only by trees through which I could make my way easily to the next bramble clump. Once or twice Grandfather Peter cautioned me not to hurry. I checked my pace only briefly for I wanted to have finished and be back at the Houses. At one point the growth gave way to a clearing strewn with gray slabs of stone through which only a few random bushes and thistles had sprung, and I realized later that we must have been passing near to where Susan and I had seen the carz. At the time I thought only of pressing on and had gone some paces beyond the clearing and was about to tackle a larger tangle when Grandfather Peter called sharply, "Wait! Don't go on!"

His command checked me just in time. I saw that only a pace in front of me the brambles masked a sudden fall in the ground so steep that it looked more like a hole than a natural tilt. It appeared to reach downwards and had a strange blackness about it.

Grandfather Peter, now close to me, panted, "Not that way! To your right, over by those holly trees."

I went the few paces, but as I was about to edge round the hollies, the Headman called, "That'll do! You wait there."

I stopped. He and Father Dennis passed me with their burden to where a few steps ahead another slab of grayish stone made a way for them around that strangely black hole. The dark cluster of holly leaves hid them from me, but as I moved to watch them, the Headman called again, "Wait there!"

I waited. I could hear the rustling of their movements but I could not make out what they were doing. I could see—though I did not take in its significance at the time—that about the place were several fragments of buildings, some built of slabs of stone, others more like rusted skeletons of house-shapes, many of them large.

For a few moments the Headman and Father Dennis must have rested, for I remember a hush seemed to settle on the place. Then I heard the Headman ask, "Ready?" and Father Dennis grunt in reply. There was a sudden movement, a kind of tearing sound, and then the stillness returned until at last I heard Father Dennis say, "That's that."

As they came back towards me I saw that Father Dennis was holding only the empty blanket. I must have started at the sight, for as he reached me Grandfather Peter put a hand on my shoulder, saying, "You're young for this. You'll come to understand that it has to be."

I almost blurted out a question, but I remembered the black-rimmed hole reaching downwards and I knew. And suddenly my mind gave a leap to another death that had happened thereabouts, and I guessed something of Grandfather Philip's mysterious end. The hole—I would have stumbled into it myself but for Grandfather Peter's warning—must have caught him.

In silence we started back but, after only a few paces, the Headman asked Father Dennis, "How near did they come? Could you show me?"

Father Dennis stood heavily puzzled for a moment or

two, but I had guessed that Grandfather Peter was referring to the strangers' intrusion into the Waste before understanding penetrated Father Dennis's slow-moving
mind. He nodded backwards, back beyond the cluster
of hollies behind which I had waited. "Only to the fallen
tree," he said.

His answer seemed not to satisfy the Headman. He
paused, uncertain what to do. I realized that he had no
wish to take me further, but to send me back alone to the
village would, after my recent experience, have been
heartless. After a moment he told me to wait where
I was and that he and Father Dennis would be gone only
a few minutes, and he added, "Remember that you have
promised secrecy. One day you will come to appreciate—
to understand—what we have to do. Just wait and ask no
questions. We'll not be long."

The holly clump prevented me from seeing clearly
what they did. I saw that they went on beyond the black-
rimmed hole, some way beyond it. And they walked
easily, not as if they were forcing a way through thickets
but as if they were following a clear path.

Guiltily, I tried to peer through the screening hollies.
I knew I was all but breaking the secrecy the Headman
had imposed, that I was trespassing into knowledge to
which, as yet, I had not been admitted. I glimpsed the
two figures—Father Dennis square and heavy, the Headman gaunt and a head taller—going on beyond the hole.
I realized that they must be walking along the "road"
Susan had spoken of and that they were passing very

near to where the carz was hidden. And yet they did not even glance towards it. Could the tangle of growth hide the ruin's telltale contents from them, or had they known —for years perhaps—that the carz was there?

I saw that they stopped where a great thicket seemed to bar their way. At first I could not make out how the "road" had so abruptly ended, and then I saw that, long ago, a great tree had fallen across it and that since then other trees and brambles and thorns had sprung up about it. The "road" was effectively barred about a hundred paces beyond the Forbidden Area.

I looked away quickly so that, as they turned back, they would not catch me watching them, but they did not return immediately. Glancing their way again I saw that Father Dennis was making gestures with his hands, spreading his arms as if to indicate that part of the Waste between the fallen tree and where the brook cut its deep, tumbling gully through the growth. It was not until afterwards that I realized that Father Dennis was planning our defenses, was suggesting a thick barrier to further intruders between where the fallen tree blocked the road and the obstacle of the brook's gully.

After a minute or two they turned to come back and I quickly looked away again; and so it was that I realized what my eyes had taken in but my mind, intent on all that had happened, had not understood. The Forbidden Area with its black hole and fragments of buildings was —could only be—what the pale strangers that John and I had met had been talking about: a place where the strange stone, the "coal," was "dug out of the ground," the stuff that made "machines" drive themselves . . . and adding a suddenly bewildering twist to the realization came the thought that the Headman and Father Dennis must have known, for years perhaps, that the coal was there. They must have known, too, enough of its significance to guess why strangers sought it. And that must have confirmed that much of what Old Carz had spoken of was true.

I can remember little of the walk back to the village. I recall that as they joined me Grandfather Peter gave me what he must have hoped was a reassuring smile; it chilled me so that I felt afraid and small as I walked between the two men across the lower pasture. Once I stumbled and the Headman put a hand on my shoulder to steady me. Instinctively I jerked myself free from the touch and only with an effort held myself from running away. Misunderstanding, he said in his unreal, gentle voice, "You're young for such an ordeal, Gerald. One day you'll understand that it has to be."

All the village was waiting for our return. As we approached the yard-gate, they parted so that we could go on into the Grandparents' House, and there we all assembled. The Headman went and stood at one end, close to his room door. Father Dennis stood stolidly at his right and the Headman beckoned me to stand at his left. Before the three of us stood the gathering of faces, sad and watchful.

At first I heard little of what Grandfather Peter said.

I was too aware of the many faces intent on us, and their very familiarity seemed to add to the tangle of my thoughts. Could all of them, I found myself wondering, have been so deceived for so long? Could none of them have realized the Headman's and Father Dennis's trickery and so detected some hints of truth in Old Carz' tales?

And then a phrase from the Headman caught my ear. He was speaking not of Old Carz as we all had known and thought of him, but of "our friend and comrade Paul before his affliction smote him." I missed a sentence or two as I realized that the Headman was referring to Old Carz' crippled foot; and by then he had gone on to talk about the old man being "the last of the Great-grandparents and so the last of those brave and adventurous people who, under the Founder's guidance, brought our thriving community into being." I was too young at the time to understand that on such an occasion one does not say all that one knows. Then, as one unreal phrase followed another, I felt myself waiting for some explanation, some hint, of why Old Carz had been passed over as Headman, of why he had become a figure of ridicule. But Grandfather Peter's smooth words omitted even to mention the long years Old Carz had lived alone in his hut, the long years in which our secluded way of living had been shaped.

When the Headman ended, others spoke. Grandfather Brian said a little for the Grandparents, and then Father Alan for the Parents. I think that perhaps Father Alan might have said more than the others, might at least have told of his childhood recollections of the old man and so have given me a clue. But he was interrupted. Little Angela, catching the sadness of the occasion though she could rarely have seen Old Carz, suddenly burst into tears. It was as if her gasping cry released the natural feelings of us all. Carole's mouth suddenly drooped and she was covering her face with her hands, and tears were trickling down Grandmother Mary's full cheeks. And then the faces before me blurred and I was struggling against a great sob, and Mother Rachel's arm was round me and her voice, gently soothing, was in my ear as it had often been when I had lived in the Parents' House.

That evening only four of us went back to the Children's House: Carole and Susan, Stephen and I. Little Angela and Patrick remained for the night in the Parents' House, where stayed also young John, still struggling with his chill.

That night I felt again desperately alone. The experiences of the day, and the realizations they had flung into my mind, seemed to be longing for utterance. And again I felt, more intensely than before, the intangible way by which each of us was kept apart from the others. Carole was already busying about the meal as if this were just any afternoon, Stephen was glumly helping her. Susan was standing at one of the little windows that peered through the thickness of the house wall into the yard.

I realize now that Susan must have chosen the place on purpose for, if we kept our voices low, the thickness of the wall would muffle our words from the others. At the time I knew only that I had to be with someone.

She did not turn to look at me, instead she rested her hand for a moment on my arm. When she spoke it was to ask, almost casually, "Was it inside the Forbidden Area, then?" Without waiting for me to answer, she went on, "He was right about the carz. Probably he has been right about other things, too. And we've not been allowed to know."

I began in a sudden whisper, "He's written—he wrote it down—"

"Yes, you told me," Susan said.

"But there's more to it," I went on. "These men in the Waste, and the ones John and I met and the black stones —'coal,' it's called—"

"That's in the Forbidden Area, too?" she asked.

I stared at her, afraid that I was blabbing about secret things, things she must never know. And then I realized I had little to tell her that she had not already guessed.

I remembered the Headman and Father Dennis walking on beyond the black hole, and Father Dennis spreading his arms to show where the way could be blocked. I said, "I think Grandfather Peter will try and stop the strangers, make some kind of defense. And before that happens, I must know! I must know if the strangers are . . . well, if they're only wanting the coal, why should Grandfather Peter be thinking to stop them? If we only knew what kind of people they are, if they're against us or—or not."

Still looking out into the yard as if we were chatting about everyday matters, Susan asked, "And you think Old Carz' writings might tell you?"

"I—I hope so. He said he was going to write down all

he could remember. There might be something, some idea of what to expect—"

"And you think from what Carole said, that he had hidden his writings above the hut, near the Wall?"

"I hope so. Carole saw him coming down and—"

Susan interrupted, "Could you read them if you found them?"

"I—I think I could. I've learned that—"

I checked myself from giving away any secret of the Reading and Writing. "But how can I get them?" I went on. "The snow would still show my footprints, and I've no reason to go to the hut. If Grandfather Peter ever came to know—"

Susan asked, "What are they like, these writings? Are they heavy to carry?"

"Oh no," I said. "They're on pa—on thin sheets, little signs on thin sheets. There may be four or five sheets."

"Then I could get them," said Susan calmly.

"You? But how—?"

"You think they're hidden in the Wall up a bit from the hut?" she asked. "He wouldn't have walked far, not with his foot."

"But how can you go there?" I asked. "If anyone saw you—"

She smiled with her head held slightly sideways, her eyebrows lifted. "That's not difficult," she said coolly. "The hut will have to be swept out and his things brought down. I'll make sure to be near when Carole is told to send someone."

Smith and the Black Stone

THE THAW MEANT that outdoor work could be resumed, but behind the usual activities there was, that spring, a feeling of urgency. The knowledge that strangers had penetrated the Waste, and that the Headman and Father Dennis saw the happening as ominous, gave us all a feeling that the essential work had to be done as quickly as possible, that we must all be prepared for whatever was to happen.

Among our tasks we children were set the clearing out of the brook before the melting snow so choked it that water spread over the lower fringes of the fields. The first possible morning we went and got the wooden rakes, but as we were about to set off Grandmother Ruth came over to us, walking stiffly for the damp had brought on her rheumatism.

"There's the old man's things," she reminded Carole. "I've not had a chance to get up to the hut."

Susan was waiting nearby. "Shall I get them?" she asked. "I could sweep out the place at the same time."

The trace of a scowl crossed Carole's face as if she resented Susan's intrusion into what she, as oldest girl, had to decide, but she realized that for herself to go to the hut would mean losing Stephen's company.

Grandmother Ruth's deeply-lined face for once softened. "That's a good girl," she said to Susan. "Take a broom with you. And don't forget to bolt the door as you come out. We don't want any animals making their lair inside."

So, as Stephen and Carole and I trudged up to where the brook struggled out from the upper pasture, Susan clambered up to the hut with a broom on her slight shoulder. I remember feeling a great relief that she had contrived to go and an admiration for the skill with which she had got the job. Her going had seemed quite natural; she even waved to us as she neared the hut.

Ever and again as the three of us toiled to free the tangles of rotten leaves and twigs and mud that the brook had brought down to choke its twisting way through the boulders, I glanced up towards the hut. I saw Susan only once, apparently busily sweeping it out. I did not see her go up beside the Wall, but I knew that if Old Carz' writings were there to be found, she would find them.

That afternoon occurred an incident that was to increase the mounting tension in the valley. We three, Carole and Stephen and I, had worked our way down below the boulders, had reached the smoother ground where the brook made a gentler way between the fields. As I worked I had struck a long obstruction, what seemed to be an endless tube of an unfamiliar kind of stone embedded in the bank of the brook. My discoveries of the past few weeks suggested that the long tube could once have led the waters trapped by the Wall—the "old dam," as Old Carz had called it—far down the valley, perhaps even to a townz miles away. The riddle of the Wall, which had long baffled me, had been answered.

But I was becoming so accustomed to finding such confirmations of Old Carz' beliefs, that I did not think long about this one. And, within a minute or two, our attention was diverted by a whistle sounding from up on the Mountain where Grandfather Brian was acting shepherd. Though the three short blasts told us that there was no alarm, we looked up as Stephen pulled out his whistle to pass the message on down the valley.

"It'll be Smith," said Carole, excitement in her voice, and soon we saw the man, riding one horse and leading the other with his equipment, come over the shoulder of the Mountain.

Smith's arrival in our valley was something of an event —though we children never approached near enough to speak with him (which, I now knew, we were forbidden to do). His first visit of the year marked the beginning of spring for us almost as much as the first call of the chiffchaff from the treetops of the Waste. We three stood, resting on our rakes, watching him coming down the path that led across the upper pasture, and waved when he looked our way.

The path led to the gap that had long ago been made through the boulders that separated the upper pasture from the valley, and from there on down to the Houses. But instead of keeping to the path, Smith this time stopped his horses and, dismounting, began to come over to us. Carole and Stephen watched him with puzzlement, I with uncertainty, but we could not ignore the man, nor could I as yet pronounce the Rule to Carole and Stephen.

The man called to us while he was still several paces away, and Carole and Stephen started towards him. I held back a moment or two, but curiosity urged me to follow.

Smith was holding out a piece of the black stone, the "coal," like that the strangers had shown John and me, like that I now knew was to be found in the Forbidden Area. The sight of it caused me to hesitate, and I recalled that thin paper with Smith's name on it.

His question surprised me. "Do you know if there's any of it about here?" he asked.

Stephen shook his head, but I stood staring at the man. If he had been into the Forbidden Area he must have known that coal was there.

Carole asked, "What is it?"

"Coal," said Smith, and I was near enough to see him more clearly than I had done before. He was smaller than I had realized, and had a thin, sharp face and almost black hair. And though he had a scant beard, his skin had the even paleness that I had seen on the other strangers.

"People burn it," he went on, nodding back the way he had come as if indicating the land beyond our Mountain. "It burns well. They've been finding they can use it to drive machines, too."

"Machines?" repeated Carole for, like John before, the word was new to her.

"Yes," Smith nodded. "And they'll pay for it, pay good money. So if you find any of it about . . ."

He must have caught the puzzlement on all our faces at the word "money." He gave a quick smile. "I was forgetting," he said. "You don't know much about such things." He flashed a glance down the valley. "I don't know how much longer people like you can live shut away," he said and, as he turned back towards his horse, he added, "Let me know if you find any of it, won't you?"

I saw why he had left us. Grandfather Peter and Father Dennis were striding up towards us. Carole, too, caught the urgency in their step. She grasped her rake and hurried back to work though Stephen, a puzzled frown on his face, watched for a few moments as Smith mounted and went on towards the Headman.

They met about halfway to the Houses. For a little while they appeared to talk, and then, as Father Dennis turned back to walk beside Smith to the village, the Headman came on to us.

We had resumed our work, and I felt rather than saw

Grandfather Peter's determined approach. I knew he would ask me what had passed between us and Smith, that he might blame me for the man having spoken to us —though I could hardly have told Stephen and Carole, both my superiors in the village's reckoning, that we were forbidden by a Rule to speak with Smith. And, more disturbing, had been Smith's question about the coal, when the thin paper with his name had been lying near the Forbidden Area. But I could tell the Headman nothing of that; it would mean confessing that Susan and I had been into the Forbidden Area ourselves.

Grandfather Peter stopped a dozen paces from us and called me to him. He stood, towering, watching my approach.

He began, "You know the Rule. Why did you speak with Smith?"

"I—I didn't," I stammered, clutching at strict accuracy.

"But I saw you! I saw you go over to him!"

I managed to protest, "I didn't say anything."

"You didn't? If you didn't, Carole and Stephen did. What did they say?"

I told him only that Smith had asked them if they had seen any of the black stone, and that both had said they had not.

"Is that all they said?" he demanded. "Did not Smith tell you why he wanted it?"

"He said something about people burning it," I ventured, but I held back Smith's mention of "machines." Though I was sure that Grandfather Peter, and Father Dennis, too, knew of the coal in the Forbidden Area, I dared not let him know what Susan and I had already guessed. Nor could I tell him that I had reason to believe that Smith knew of the coal, too. I met the Headman's piercing stare more boldly than I felt, almost as if I was facing not an aging man whom all my life I had accepted as the greatest among us, but rather as someone nearer an enemy.

"And was that all he said?" he asked.

I added, "He said something about paying money for the stone. I don't know what he meant."

At least I was keeping within the truth and my admission about "money"—true at that time—seemed to soften his attitude.

"But you said nothing," he persisted, "nothing about having seen this—this black stone."

"No," I said. "He asked Carole and Stephen, and they said they hadn't seen it."

He waited a long moment before asking, "And what would you have said if he had asked you?"

I guessed what was in his mind. He did not want to tell me of the coal in the Forbidden Area if I had not noticed it. I evaded the answer he was seeking.

"I'd have told him about the strangers showing John and me," I said.

His look sharpened at once. "What's that? You have spoken with strangers about the—the black stone?"

I replied quickly, "John told you at the time. It was when Grandfather Tony twisted his foot at the hunting. . . ."

I think he had forgotten the incident. I had to tell him

of it afresh, but, aware that I had guided his thoughts away from Smith, and from what I had seen in the Forbidden Area, too, I felt a little less uneasy. I did not say anything about what the pale strangers—and Smith, too—had hinted of the uses of the coal.

At last Grandfather Peter appeared satisfied. "You have done the right thing," he said with his uneasy smile. "We don't want such strangers in our valley, do we? They are bad men. No, not bad—misguided would be a fairer word. They do not know the evil they and their black stone can cause. It was such men with such ideas that brought about the Upheaval long ago. Did you know that?"

I said, "No," even though my growing belief in Old Carz' tales had hinted of such a possibility. Indeed, standing before the Headman, I felt again uncertain, again fearful of where our discoveries—Susan's and mine—might lead. Had I not come to distrust Grandfather Peter, I might even at that late time have told him what I had found out, but I knew that I had passed the point where I could go back to accepting him and his ideas without question.

He smiled again as if he assumed that I agreed with him. "We must live in our way," he said, and again I caught, above the curve of his little mouth, his unsmiling, watchful eyes. Again he appeared to be trying to reassure me and to make certain I accepted his words, and yet I felt that deep down he was unsure of himself and of his own beliefs.

"Well, back to work," he added, and turned abruptly towards the village.

At some time, perhaps when Smith had been talking to Carole and Stephen, perhaps when the Headman had been questioning me, Susan must have gone from Old Carz' hut back to the village. When we three returned we found her already there preparing the meal. Carole was, I remember, relieved that it was nearly ready. "That cleaning out the brook!" she said. "It's the worst job!"

Susan said, "The meal won't be long, and then"—she flashed a glance at me—"you'll be able to get on to your bunks and have a rest, won't you?"

She spoke as she always did, but that quick glance had told me: she had found Old Carz' writings and had hidden them in my bunk.

I had to wait long hours before I dared to try and get the writings. Not until I could be sure everyone in the House was asleep, the girls at their end as well as John and little Patrick and Stephen, did I risk sliding my hand under the mattress. Never had I realized that paper rustled, and how loudly in the sleeping House. But I drew it out, three sheets of it, on which I could see by the fire's glow were lines of writing. I slipped the sheets under my tunic and, in time, fell asleep. The next morning I awoke at the first movement and the writing was so much on my mind that I immediately felt the sheets with my fingers.

I had another wait before I could even look at them in the seclusion of the latrine; and there disappointment met me, for they were written in the small, linked writing I had glimpsed when I had seen Old Carz at work, and there was not a word I recognized. The Rules were written only in what I have learned are called block capital letters and crudely shaped, I knew as yet nothing of small letters or of joining them into words. I doubt if I would have tried to unravel their mysteries had not the old man headed one sheet: BEFORE THE FOUNDATION. That at least told me his way of writing capitals, and a quick search showed among his small letters some of similar shape to his large ones. But those were the only clues.

During the next few days I tried to find opportunities to study Old Carz' writing; but they were days full of work, and of work that we all undertook with growing urgency. Rumors began to spread through our little community: strange sounds had been heard coming from the Waste, unexplained footprints had been seen, unfamiliar voices were said to have been heard in the distance. Never before had we known how such hints of danger—real or imagined—could so take hold of ordinary, familiar people.

Grandfather Peter took the lead in what was coming to look like our defense. I think that Smith's words with Carole and Stephen and me about the black stones had urged the Headman into action. Within a day or two of Smith's departure, work was reorganized in a way that we had never known before. All the outdoor work that could possibly be undertaken by the Mothers and Grandmothers was passed over to them; I remember seeing Grandmother Ruth guiding the harrow for the spring preparation while Grandmother Mary and Mother Rachel toiled to pull it and, later, Mother Janet and Mother Mavis sowing the oats. Meanwhile John was dispatched to act as shepherd for the day, leaving Carole, Susan and me, and even Angela and Patrick, to take over the work on the Vegetables, the squarish patch behind the barn where early sowings of carrots and turnip and broad beans and suchlike were waiting to be done. All the men, except for Grandfather Tony whose ankle was still hindering him, took to setting off each daybreak into the Waste, armed with axes and sickles and saws. The sounds that soon began to come from there and were to persist through several days, told of trees being felled and branches cut. It became clear that some kind of barricade was being constructed—and, indeed, it was soon generally known that the men were intent on closing access through the Waste to any more intruders who might appear. I guessed that the slope between the long-fallen tree barring the old road and the deep gully of the brook was being thickly fenced—and Stephen confirmed my guess when at dusk he returned with the men. By his account a thick fence of impenetrable thorn was already well started.

In all this disturbance of our usual steady pace of working, we children who were left under Grandfather Tony's command found ourselves frequently changing jobs; and at times Susan and I worked side by side—sowing carrots, perhaps, or setting shallots—so that we could now and again talk without fear of being overheard. Two or three times Susan asked how I was getting on with puzzling out Old Carz' writings. I had to confess that I had made very little headway. "And I must understand it," I added in a whisper. "We must know what it is these invaders are after. If it is only the coal, why should Grandfather Peter and the others be so alarmed? Why not let them come and take it?"

Susan asked why I had made so little progress with the writing and I told her something of my difficulties with Old Carz' small, linked letters. "If I could only write them out in the letters I've learned, I think I could get on quicker."

"Could you do that?" she asked, with a sideways glance to make sure that little Angela was not near enough to hear us.

I felt sure I could do it. I could make up a paste of soot and water easily enough, and find a stick or a reed for the writing; and I had noticed that Old Carz had so spread his neat, tight lines of writing that there were spaces for my clumsier letters between them. If I could write in those spaces all the letters I had already discovered—instead of trying to hold them in my memory from one hurried glance to the next—the matter would begin to take shape. No doubt there would be words that would baffle me, but I could at least hope to understand enough. . . .

"How long would it take?" Susan asked.

"That's the trouble," I replied. "It might only take a day if I could just get on with it. But having to hide the writings away every time someone looks my way, and having to stop just when I'm beginning to understand a few words, and then I've forgotten them when I get the next chance to look . . ."

She nodded. She knew enough of the writing—she had

gathered it from what I had already hinted, not from my telling her directly of the secrets of the Headman's room —to be able to guess at my difficulties.

"And at any time the strangers might come," I added.

Neither she nor I, nor probably any of us in the village, had really thought what might happen if and when the invaders came. We could hope that our defenses, the product of Father Dennis's ideas, would discourage a small party, but if many came, and if they brought their axes and sickles and made a really determined attack . . . so long had we lived in seclusion that such a possibility was beyond our imagination.

"So the sooner you sort out Old Carz' writings," Susan went on practically, "the sooner we may know what to expect. That's what you mean, isn't it?"

I nodded, glancing around to make sure that Carole and Patrick were still too far away to hear us. "And I can't sort it out if I have to keep changing from one job to another, and if there's always someone around who might ask what I'm doing. If I could only get time to myself somewhere—up at the shepherd's hut, for instance, or—"

"Why not?" asked Susan. "When Grandfather Tony arranges the work tomorrow, why couldn't you go up there instead of John?"

It proved quite easy to contrive. The next morning, after the men, with Stephen, had set out again for their defensive work in the Waste, and Grandfather Tony, still limping, was making up his mind what work the

Mothers should do, and what we children should be set to, Susan said calmly, "John can help me with the peas. That'll leave Gerald to act the shepherd for the day."

Grandfather Tony, already bewildered by the unfamiliar task of organizing the work, did not even query the suggestion. We just set off on our tasks, gathering such tools as we needed—and for me, secretly, a mug and a handful of soot snatched from over the fire. I found a few thin sticks on the way up, and water to make my paste for writing was at hand in the spring below the shepherd's hut.

Squatting at the door of the hut with the flock below me and a full view of the valley so that I was not likely to be surprised, I took out from under my tunic the first sheet of Old Carz' writing and set to work. In my haste it took me an annoyingly long time to mix the soot and water so that the paste would flow freely and yet not blot, and my fingers fumbled as I tried to whittle a fine point to my sticks. But at last I could begin to write my crude letters under such of Old Carz' small ones as I could recognize. . . .

That was to prove an exasperating morning. Understanding came far slower and more laboriously than I had expected. I started working word by word but, though I felt a thrill as a word or two in the first few lines took shape, before I had finished the short opening paragraph I had become aware that there were still so many blanks that I could read none of it. I stared at my little efforts in dismay, below them stretched many more lines, all mysterious to me. To read Old Carz' writings would take not hours, as I had imagined, but days—if I could do it at all.

As I stared, a half-familiar shape caught my eye from lower down the page: a word that looked like "people" which had been my first clue to the discovery that letters had sounds. The two *p*'s, I saw, were in the right places, and so was the *o*. For a moment I hardly dared to hope that the two little loops, so unlike the capital letters I had learned, could be Old Carz' way of writing the letter *e*. But the loops came in the right places in the word. . . .

Hopeful again, I began searching through his many lines for the same letter-shape; and then, on a thought, I went through the whole page writing under his neat, linked letters all those I could recognize. With growing excitement, I saw whole words here and there appear. . . .

But when at last I had worked through the page and tried to discover a meaning among the words and part-words, bafflement returned. It was not only that the skills of reading and writing were still very new to me, the little I had learned in the Headman's room had scarcely prepared me for all the puzzling ways of spelling even common words. It must, at times, have taken me a full minute to recognize a word that I knew, to discover that "town" was so spelled and not "townz" as we had always said, that "road" had, oddly, an *a* in it, that "fire" ended with an inexplicable *e*. And linking such words were many more that, even when I had all or nearly all the letters, were still unknown to me.

My excitement ebbing, I returned to the old man's opening lines, and began struggling to find a meaning in them. Even the first words seemed beyond me: "I was orn in Ru y, ut w ile still a a y my fat er too me . . ." I must have stared at that line a dozen times before I recognized his letter *b* and saw that Old Carz had started with his birth. This realization guided me to some understanding of his opening lines. And from them, as with suddenly reviving hope I filled in more of the missing letters, I could glimpse something of what followed.

I became so engrossed in the task that I all but forgot to look up from time to time to check that the sheep were not wandering too far or to make sure that no one was approaching up the valley. Once I was concerned to see that the sun, peering between clouds, had already reached behind the Forbidden Area and so I knew that noon had passed. But I reckoned I had as yet little to fear; not until dusk would whichever of the Fathers had the night watch as shepherd start the long walk. And already I had found that Old Carz had begun with an account of his early childhood, probably, as he could have been only four or five at the time of the Upheaval, based on what the Founder had told him.

As I pressed on, I realized that he had continued with the story that all of us had long known, of how the Founder (whom he called "Uncle") had taken him on the journey that had ended in our valley, being joined by four other children on the way. But though I knew the outline of the story, Old Carz' telling had a vividness and a reality that were startlingly new to me.

It seemed that the Founder and the children had walked only at night as if they had feared to be noticed; for the old man had written of houses and "whole streets" being burned, of roads "blown up," and of hiding by day in ruined buildings. And even after they had reached what he called "the country"—it seemed that the town had sprawled over such a vast area that fields were far distant from it—they had found no safety. They had, he told, often to hide from "gangs." At first I took that word to mean wild animals of some kind, until he wrote of "gangs" raiding farms and stealing crops from the fields as well as from the barns and even using as food the stored seed grain, and slaughtering all the stock to eat instead of keeping some to breed from. By then I had realized that "gangs" meant some kind of wild people; and at once I guessed that their incredible stupidity must have been an expression of the madness that had brought on the Upheaval. And he told that these gangs fought among themselves; once he had seen such a fight, ending in the deaths of two men and a child, which had sprung up over the carcass of a single cow. But here and there were phrases which, even after I had made out the words, were beyond my understanding: he wrote of food being scarce "because none was reaching the shops," and of "hospitals" being unable to "deal with the thousands of injured," and of flames "spreading from street to street" and "firefighters" made helpless because the "water supply" had been damaged. And yet, though the unfamiliar words prevented my knowing exactly what he meant, Old Carz' writing conveyed to me the feeling that, even after eighty years, his early fears had remained alive in his memory.

Late though it was, I felt impelled to turn to the next

sheet, but I could not concentrate on it. Instead I kept wondering what madness could have so seized the people that they had eaten the animals they needed to keep their villages going and the seed that they must have known they had to sow if they were to avoid hunger. And, as I sat trying to snatch some wisp of understanding, I saw far down the valley the men returning from the Waste.

I thrust the sheets of writing under my tunic, but my mind still ran on the story, and I felt myself struggling again between a desire to know and a fear of where knowing might lead. Could it be that, in spite of all Susan and I had discovered, in spite of what seemed the Headman's deliberate deception, those who had shaped our secluded way of living were right? Could Father Dennis and the others I could see coming back from the threatened Waste be building a defense against a repetition of the appalling story that Old Carz had told?

I could only hope that the next pages of his writings would at least give me some answers to the questions that were crowding in on me as I saw Father Harold start up the path to take over the sheep watching for the night.

The Old Ways

PERHAPS IT WAS FORTUNATE that all of us in the Children's House were so tired that evening that we had little to say to one another and went early and willingly to our bunks. Had I had an opportunity to tell Susan even a little of the fearsome story that Old Carz had started to tell, I might have passed on to her my new uncertainties. As it was, I felt so weary in my mind from trying to understand that, to my later surprise, I fell asleep quickly and did not awake next morning until after the others were up.

The new, fear-charged pattern of work was repeated that day. The men and Stephen set off to the Waste through the growing light of an overcast morning, the

Mothers and Grandmothers took over all the outdoor work they could, even Mother Mavis carrying her two-month-old Andrew on her back; and Carole, Susan, John and the two little ones went again to the Vegetables to clear the ground in readiness for the planting out and late sowings that would soon be needed. And I set off again to act the shepherd, following Susan's lead, I appointed myself while Grandfather Tony still stared around in bewilderment.

As soon as I had seen that all was well—the sheep seemed content to nibble close by the protecting wall along the mountain ridge—I made my paste, sharpened a stick or two, and took out the second sheet of Old Carz' writing. As before I worked quickly, writing my clumsy letters in the spaces between his lines. But after perhaps a half-hour of such working I began to realize that he had not continued the story he had started on the sheet I had puzzled out the day before. A more explanatory note had crept in—I caught it here and there as I managed to put together a phrase or two. By the time I had reached the bottom of the page I knew that he had written not a continuation of his story but, rather, an explanation of how people had lived in the Old Days.

He must have written as simply as he could, as if to explain to me, but even more than on the first sheet, I found many words and phrases that baffled me. He wrote almost entirely about people living in towns and working in "factories and offices"—whatever they were. Never once did he tell of the townspeople gathering their har-

vests or tending their animals. Indeed, he seemed to imply
that they had a curious means of obtaining their food in
the town itself; I recalled his talking about "shopz,"
though how the food could have been grown in them I
could not guess.

And through the whole page kept recurring two bewildering words: "trade" and "money." I wondered if
they could have been grown in shopz, too, until I remembered Smith speaking of "money" as if it could be exchanged for coal; and indeed Old Carz, on the page I had
already read, had written of food "not reaching the
shops." "Money," it seemed, and "trade" could not be
foods and yet, as the Upheaval came nearer, both seemed
to become scarce—or, as the old man put it, "trade
dwindled" and "money became almost useless." And,
even more bewildering, Old Carz once wrote of the "business of the country" being linked with "seaborne trade";
I could not see at all how the fields and pastures that for
me made up "the country" could have any connection
with the sea which, from what Grandmother Mary had
once said, I imagined to be a watery continuation of the
sky below the horizon.

Not until I was nearing the end of that daylong
struggle did I gain any understanding of what Old Carz
had been trying to tell me. For hours I seemed to have
to cling to the hope that there was truth in his bewildering phrases, as Susan and I had found truth in his notion
of a carz. Indeed it was my mental linking of the two—the
old man's writing of people obtaining food in a town and

our discovery of the carz—that gave me the first wisp of understanding. For I realized that the men who had made the carz would have needed time as well as their incredible skills. From the little that Susan and I had seen I could guess that the carz had not been made in occasional half days like the winter afternoons we spent repairing our tools or making our simple furniture; and then the makers would have needed even more time to devise the means by which the carz would move itself. It could have taken days and weeks of working during which the makers would have had little time to help in the fields or thresh the grain or even to do such weeding as we children often did. They, the makers of a carz, must have had other people to do the essential work, and people who would be willing to exchange some of their harvest for the finished carz. And if there were enough people who wanted a carz, and who could spare grain or meat in payment, there could have been many makers of carz, dozens of them perhaps, living not in a village like ours but in—

Old Carz' other tales—of the boxes in which you could see miles away, of people flying in air carz—came bounding up from my memory; and I suddenly realized that there could have been people spending their working time on such wonders, too. And to bring them to the villages where they exchanged them for the food they had not time to grow for themselves, they would need not rough paths like that alongside our brook, but smooth "roads" like that out in the forest.

I felt other scarcely credible possibilities spreading out from such ideas. As yet I could not begin to guess where the black coal fitted in, or what that strange word "money" meant, or how some of the townmade wonders could be exchanged with people who lived hundreds of miles away. But I began to discern a connection between such a very strange way of living and the Upheaval that had brought it to an end. For Old Carz' first sheet of writing had implied that the Upheaval had started in the towns, which suggested that it must have been the makers of carz and "seeing boxes" and other wonders who had begun it. Perhaps they had been unable to find anyone to supply them with the food they had not time to produce. Then hunger would have faced them, and so they would have been driven to find what food they could, to steal, even to eat the seed grain and the young stock. . . .

Could that be, I suddenly wondered, what the strangers who were now threatening to invade us from the Waste were after? Could they be makers of carz who were now, driven by the threat of starvation, intent on stealing our stores? But even as the fear came to me, I knew it to be false. The pale strangers whom John and I had met on the second hunt had not looked hungry men; they had had horses and the cloth of their tunics was finer than the Grandmothers wove. And yet, somehow, they were involved with the Old Ways; the Headman's words to me after Smith had spoken with Carole and Stephen clearly linked their seeking coal with the appalling Upheaval. And now they were threatening to invade our Waste for it.

Bewilderment began to seize me again. No sooner had

I glimpsed a possible answer to one question than a dozen more were flooding into my mind. I sat staring down the valley with unseeing eyes, struggling to understand, unaware that through the thickening twilight a figure was approaching me, was only a few paces away—

"So that is how you keep watch!"

I jumped up guiltily, trying to hide the sheet of writing, but I think that even in my alarm I was relieved that it was Father Alan who had caught me.

He saw the paper. "What is that you have?" he asked.

"It's writing," I said.

He looked down at the sheet. He said, "But that is not like the Headman has. What is it? Where did you get it?"

He sounded not angry or alarmed, but curious.

I hesitated, and then told him that it was Old Carz' writing, and, as he still did not show anger or alarm, I went on, "He wrote it down so that I—someone—should know about how people lived in the Old Days. They had machines that did strange things and—"

"Carz?" he asked, "and suchlike?"

There was no mockery in his tone, and no hint of disapproval or of concern that I might be sharing Old Carz' fantasies.

"Yes," I ventured and, as again he showed no surprise, I went on, "There were such things. I know there were because we found—"

I stopped myself, remembering almost too late that I was risking implicating Susan.

In his same quiet tone Father Alan said, "Yes, I know

there were." And as I stared in astonishment, he nodded towards the far side of the Mountain, where the forest reached out. "We have found them when we've been hunting."

"You know!" I blurted, relief and something near to anger mingling in my voice. "And the Headman and Father Dennis—do they know too?"

"Probably," he said.

"But why? Why did they pretend Old Carz was mad? Why didn't they tell—?"

"Think, lad, of the Upheaval they brought," he interrupted gently. "Peter reckoned—or, really, it was Grandfather Robert before him—that they would bring back the Upheaval, that people would become so much set on carz and such things, and turn away from doing the work . . ."

"Why should they?" I had to ask, and, as another thought suddenly struck me, "If a carz can carry people, it could pull a plow and—and other things."

Through the growing dusk I caught his smile and knew that the same idea had occurred to him. He said, "It's getting dark and time you were back at your House. But I'll come part of the way with you and try to explain as we go."

As we began down the path that led across the upper pasture, he said, "I don't rightly understand it all, perhaps you can help me a bit from what Old Carz has written. But it seems that people in the Old Days came to rely on the things they made and did not grow their own food, and so it was that, when food became scarce, they fought one another—"

"He says that," I interrupted, holding out the sheet of Old Carz' writing. "He tells about that."

Father Alan looked at me sideways. "You'd better hide that writing before you get back," he warned. Then he went on, "But does he tell how it came about? Does he tell how it was that some people grew the food and others made carz and suchlike? It's always puzzled me . . ."

I tried to tell him what I had gathered from Old Carz' second sheet. It was still very jumbled in my mind but in the telling, in putting into words the thoughts that were jostling so confusedly in my mind, some of the impressions became clearer. And they must have become clearer to Father Alan, too, as he listened. As I was trying to tell how the people who made a carz had apparently exchanged it for food, he exclaimed, "So that's where the money came in!"

I still could not understand. He went on, "It was pieces of metal and—and paper, too, I've heard. And people used to exchange it for what they wanted. I remember overhearing Grandfather Philip talking to Smith about it. He wanted us to give him money for his work, not a side of mutton or a sack of grain. And he said something about being able to buy what he wanted with it."

In Father Alan's tone, usually so gentle, there was an excitement matching that I was feeling.

"What happened?" I asked.

"I don't rightly remember," he said. "I was still living

in the Children's House and I couldn't understand. But I remember that Grandfather Robert—he was Headman then—thought poorly of getting little pieces of metal for our good grain, and that he was angry with Philip about it. Or that may have been another time when a stranger had come along, and Philip had given him oats for his horse, and some cheese and bread, too, and the man had given him the metal, the money, in exchange. Most of us reckoned Philip had been daft, and some said it was the Reading and Writing that was upsetting him. . . ."

We were nearing the bottom of the upper pasture where the path led on to the village. Father Alan asked, "What else does Old Carz tell? Does he tell how the Upheaval began?"

"I've not read it all," I told him. "I'm not sure . . ."

"Keep it to yourself, lad," he said. "I'll ask you again when you've read it all. A lot may depend on it."

I knew that in a few more paces he would have to turn back to the shepherd's hut and I would have to go on alone to the village.

I asked, "What's going to happen? If the invaders come up the Waste, if they break through the fence or—or—"

Father Alan shook his head. "Who's to tell? It may be only the coal they're after." As I started with surprise at his mention of coal, I heard the smile in his voice as he went on, "Many of us have guessed that's what they're wanting. If that's all there is to it, we could give to to them, and welcome. But"—his tone became more serious— "if it's more than that, if they are truly invaders trying to steal our land and our food, what then? So much will depend on the kind of men they are, and how they come. Let's hope that by then you'll have puzzled out what Old Carz had to say. . . . It's time you were down at your House, and I was seeing that the sheep haven't gone wandering."

I reached the House far easier in my mind than I had felt for a long while, indeed, I felt so relieved that Father Alan had understood that I think I would have blurted it all out to Susan had there been any opportunity. But already Angela and Patrick were in their bunks and Carole was ill-tempered that I was late for the meal, and there was no chance to say a word to Susan.

Stephen was ill-tempered, too. He said something about my having had an easy day up on the Mountain while he, as a man, had been working at our defenses. "And we've made it that thick and thorny that they'll never force it," he added. "Another day and it'll keep anyone out."

Another day, I thought, and I may have finished Old Carz' tale and perhaps will understand.

As on the previous day I appointed myself shepherd as soon as the men had gone to the Waste and the others had set about their urgent tasks. Young John protested that it was his turn to act the shepherd, but Susan quickly told him that they were setting more peas. "And you always like doing that," she said.

That third sheet of Old Carz' writing was, at first, even more confusing than the others had been. Though I had come to find his tight letters easier to make out, and though I was quicker at recognizing words and whole phrases, I found that, as on the second page, he had not followed what had gone before. It was not until I had unravelled parts of the earlier lines that I realized I was dealing with the writing that, long ago it now seemed, he had begun to read to me when last I had visited his hut. And he seemed to have written it apart from the rest of the page. It took a long while and much puzzling before I realized that he had written this last page, or at least the opening lines of it, before what I had already read. He must have started off with what he really wanted to tell; and then, realizing that much of it would be incomprehensible to me until I knew how people had formerly lived, he had started again on another sheet to tell his story and give his explanation. And, making another difficulty for me, he must have seen that his few sheets of paper were running out and so had added the end of his account of the Upheaval in the space left unused on what had been originally his first page.

So it was that, though I deciphered much of the opening lines of that last sheet, I paid little attention to them when I discovered that, lower down the page, he had continued the story I had already begun to understand. It was on those lines that I concentrated though today I kept a more careful watch on the path up from the valley.

I could not make out all that Old Carz had to tell of the causes of the Upheaval; but I found much that I had not realized before. The Upheaval had not, as we had been told, come as a sudden madness occupying only a matter of days or weeks; it was, rather, spread over years and was brought about not by a single event but by a series of separate happenings. And those happenings, destructive though they were, had not been intended to bring about the Upheaval. Even now I can picture only a little of what must have occurred. It seems that groups of people, "rioters" or "reformers," Old Carz called them, had become dissatisfied with the way they were living and had thought to put matters right—to demand to live somehow better than the strange "money" would allow, or to help those somehow "oppressed"—by starting an "incident." That word seemed to mean doing something to upset other people, to draw attention to what the "rioters" believed wrong; it might be blocking a road, or damaging a "factory" (some kind of building), or "putting out of action waterworks and electricity stations"— whatever they were. I could not make out whether the old man agreed with such people or not. At one point he would be suggesting that they were trying to do good— "to put right what they believed to be wrong," he wrote —and in almost the next line he would be telling how they had "taken to violence," and seemed to be linking them with the "gangs" who had burned and stolen and destroyed.

Though many words still puzzled me, I could fit much of what Old Carz told to what I had already read and even to my own little knowledge. His reference to the "waterworks" being "put out of action" not only reminded me of the "dam" above our village; I recalled, also, a summer five years earlier when our brook had all but run dry and our oats had grown so poorly that we had to kill off most of our stock and those we contrived to keep through a cheerless, hungry winter had become poor, scrawny beasts. By imagining not our village but a town with thousands of people having to live perhaps a whole season almost without water, I could glimpse a little of what life during the Upheaval had been like. And when the old man told of illnesses on "so wide a scale that the health services were unable to control them," though his exact meaning eluded me, I could recall the sores and festering wounds and sicknesses that had afflicted many of us during that long, almost waterless summer.

Stretching my imagination even further, visualizing hundreds and hundreds of people so suffering and, at the same time, depending on faraway places for their food and other necessities . . . and Old Carz' tale of the Upheaval, of the stealing and raiding and killing, formed a coherent pattern. Much, I knew, was still far beyond my understanding; I could not, for instance, even guess at what he had meant by such happenings "on a worldwide scale." But I knew clearly enough why the Founder had sought refuge for the Great-grandparents in our hidden valley; and I felt a belated understanding, still restrained by my distrust of the man, why Grandfather Peter—and Grandfather Robert before him, Father Alan had said—feared close contact with the strangers who lived beyond our Mountain and our Waste.

It must have been about then, before I looked again at

the lines with which Old Carz had in fact begun his Writings, that I chanced to look down the valley. I saw that the men were coming back from the Waste though the afternoon light had not begun to fade. I guessed that they reckoned our defenses completed. I quickly put the old man's writings under my tunic; I could not hope that, if I was discovered with them again, I would meet with such understanding as Father Alan had shown.

I had a long wait before I saw Father Timothy coming up to relieve me. I must have spent the time turning over in my mind all that I had gathered from Old Carz' story. Clearly, in the Old Days people had lived more richly than we could ever hope to do; and yet their way of life had brought on the fearful Upheaval. Would the strangers, when they came, bring the benefits or the miseries of those times?

When at last I reached the village, I met Susan filling a bucket from the brook. She must have watched for me so that we could have a few words without being overheard.

"Have you finished it?" she asked, and when I nodded in reply, "What does he say?"

"There's so much of it," I replied. "They lived so strangely and yet . . ." It was impossible to put in a few snatched words all my tangled impressions. I could only repeat Father Alan's reaction: "It depends on how they come and what kind of people they are. They may be only after the coal; but if they're wanting to live like in the Old Days, if they're after our stores and our land? . . ."

We had reached the yard-gate. Susan looked at me, uncertainty clear in her eyes. But neither of us doubted that they would come, and soon. . . .

The Invasion

FIVE DAYS LATER the invaders came.

During that interval the spring work went on much as usual—at least, on the surface. Underneath we all knew that it was only a matter of time before the pale strangers returned to the Waste.

Few of us could hide our concern. The Headman at first went more about among us, reassuring us that if we showed ourselves determined and united, the strangers would go away; but though his tight mouth twisted in the smile I had come to know, as ever his little eyes remained sharp and watchful as if he felt unsure. Father Dennis supported him with dour determination. Whatever work he did during those days he always had his hunting club with him, and his heavy jaw seemed to thrust forward more than ever. Grandfather Tony became even more timorous, Grandmother Mary's smile wavered, nearly all looked anxious. As I remember, only Father Alan seemed little moved; he went calmly about the work, but there was a more thoughtful cast to his face.

He it was who raised a question which must have occurred to many of us and yet none had so far dared to face.

"What if many of them come?" he asked Father Dennis.

Father Dennis looked sullenly indignant, as if Father Alan was questioning the defenses that Dennis had taken a large part in constructing. "A dozen of them would never get through," he said, heavily stressing each word.

"There may be more than a dozen," Father Alan said quietly. "There may be hundreds of them."

"Hundreds?" echoed Father Dennis, appearing scarcely to understand so large a number. "Where would they get these hundreds from? How many villages of these strangers are there, do you think?"

"I don't know," replied Father Alan steadily. "But I've heard tell that in the old days several hundred of them lived in a townz."

Father Dennis snorted his indignation at such a suggestion, and turned away in disgust—much as he had turned away from Old Carz when he disbelieved him. And I found myself thinking that Father Dennis was, of us all, the most wrapped in ignorance. He knew of the coal in the Forbidden Area, and of the strange trackway through the forest; he must have seen a dozen, a hundred, hints that Old Carz' tales had had at least a basis of truth; and yet he had persistently refused to accept anything that disturbed his way of thinking.

During those waiting days, Father Dennis seemed to take the lead. Often he talked with the Headman, but I doubt if it was to ask his advice, more likely it was to tell him what to do. It was Father Dennis who suggested, after the completion of the barricade, another depature from our customary way of working: the appointment of a continuous watch below the threatened Forbidden Area. By day one of the Grandfathers was to watch, by night two of the Fathers, and at the first hint of danger, all of us were to gather with our hunting clubs or such tools as seemed best, behind our defenses.

There were two or three false alarms. Grandfather Tony was the first to blow the warning, and we all grasped our weapons and under Father Dennis's leadership hurried into the Waste. That we were passing close by the Forbidden Area with its skeletons of iron-framed buildings and the half-tumbled ruin that hid the carz seemed to matter little, though the Headman stationed himself near the black hole as if to keep us away from it.

Nothing happened. It seemed that Grandfather Tony had seen a strange movement, his description was so vague that it could have been no more than a few pigs nosing about or a wild dog on the prowl. After perhaps half an hour we returned. I had meanwhile seen for the first time how thoroughly our defenses had been constructed. A kind of wall, a full yard thick, of tightly woven thorn branches stretched from where the fallen tree blocked the road to the brook's gully—and that steep slope had been made even steeper and harder to climb. Even though I saw it would be possible for a man or two to scramble along the bed of the brook, or perhaps to force a way through the dense thicket that had long ago sprung up above the fallen tree, any attackers would have to come singly and the dozen of us could easily tackle them. The Headman, or more truly Father Dennis, had planned our defenses as thoroughly as time and our equipment had allowed.

Two days later, in Grandfather Kenneth's watch, the alarm was again whistled to us, and again we grabbed up our weapons and hurried into the Waste. The alarm was more justified for, even before we reached Grandfather Kenneth, we could hear from far down in the Waste strange and certainly non-animal noises. There was a kind of distant clanking, accompanied as well as we could hear by a hissing sound; and now and again we heard what sounded like a distant crashing through the growth of the Waste. We looked at one another in alarm and, though none of us uttered the word, the possibility of a carz must have come to many minds. I recall that Susan, who like most of the women had followed at a distance, looked quickly towards the ruin, all but hidden behind a thicket, in which we had found the carz. But I could not imagine that rusted box-on-wheels forcing its way through our stout, thorny barricade.

For the best part of an hour we listened to the strange sounds. For minutes at a time they would stop and the normal hush of the Waste would return; and then they started again. They seemed, at first, to be coming gradually nearer, but they were still too distant to be sure. At last, after several long minutes had passed without hearing the sounds, we went back to our work—all except Grandfather Kenneth whose watch it was, and Father Dennis who, apparently on his own decision, determined to "see if anything more happened." But when he returned in the late afternoon he had nothing further to report.

Then, after another false alarm—though it had been prompted by the same strange, distant clanking—they came. Grandfather Brian's whistle seemed to have taken on a shriller, more urgent note, and we all hurried to the threatened defenses below the Forbidden Area, Father Dennis walking doggedly in front, the Headman, his stride seeming a little less assured than usual, a pace or two behind.

Even before we had reached Grandfather Brian, we had no doubt that his alarm was truly based. He was pointing, waving, towards the trackway, the road that had once come up through the Waste and must have led directly to the Forbidden Area before the fallen tree had blocked it. And coming up that trackway were five men, mounted on horses, while somewhere in the distance behind them we could hear, more clearly than before, the strange clanking, hissing sounds—though they stopped as the strangers saw us gathering.

A dozen or so paces from the obstruction of the fallen tree the five horsemen drew up. I noticed that all of them had the paler, unbearded faces that had distinguished the strangers John and I had met, and the very dark hair; and that, as before, their tunics and trews appeared even at a distance of the same smooth cloth. One of them looked like the man who had spoken with John and me.

For a space we stood watching them, and they us. Our Fathers and Grandfathers were taking tighter hold on their hunting clubs, and I noticed that Father Timothy and Father Harold edged behind the thorn fence as if in readiness for an attack through its formidable thickness.

But it seemed that the strangers were not yet intent on attacking us. They just sat on their horses, looking a little puzzled. Then the leading man pointed past us and said something to another of them as if indicating the Forbidden Area.

At the stranger's movement Father Dennis thrust himself forward, his hunting club gripped hard. "This is our land!" he shouted.

For a long moment their leader regarded him, the hint of a smile on his pale, smooth face. Then, with a word to the others, he rode alone the few paces to where the fallen tree barred the road.

He asked, "How far does your land reach then?" and I caught the faint singsong in his voice like that of the other pale strangers.

He had spoken not to Father Dennis standing nearest him, but to Grandfather Peter a pace or two back.

The Headman replied, "The whole valley."

"As far as that?" the stranger asked. He smiled. "My name, by the way, is Rhys, and we come from down below." With a tilt of his dark head he indicated the land that stretched—how far we did not know—below the Waste. But easily as he spoke, the stranger's dark eyes were taking in the line of our defenses. Most of us guessed that he was about to order an attack, that at any moment the five of them would be trying to force their horses through at us. But the stranger said, in the same gentle, lilting voice, "It looks as if you have only recently blocked this way, as if only recently you have claimed this land."

The truth of that caused a frown to tighten the Headman's face. He began, "We have used this land since the Foundation . . ."

Again Father Dennis took the lead. "It's always been ours!" he growled. "You'd better not try to take it. There are a dozen of us to the five of you, even though you've got horses!"

The stranger Rhys looked down at him, "We are not after your land," he began, speaking slowly and distinctly. "It looks as if there was coal up there"—he gave a look towards the Forbidden Area—"and we would like to see, to make sure. If there should be coal—"

"No one goes there!" shouted Father Dennis angrily. "That's our Forbidden Area. No one goes there!"

The man Rhys waited a moment before he spoke again, and then he looked over Father Dennis's head and spoke to Grandfather Peter.

"I don't think you understand," he said. "We do not want to take your land or to interfere with how you have chosen to live. We merely want to look. There was good coal somewhere around here and we've been searching—"

"Coal!" Father Dennis spat out the word. "We know what coal did in the old days! We know about the Upheaval! We don't want none of that!"

Again the man Rhys waited, and again he spoke to the Headman. "If there is any coal there, we'll pay, of course. And if we should do any damage, we'll make that good—"

"Pay? Damage?" shouted Father Dennis, and his voice sounded the more angry at the Headman's apparent lack of support. "And what will you pay in? In those pieces of metal that are no use to us? And as for damage, you're not getting nearer!"

At that moment a murmur ran through the dozen of us on our side of the defenses. I had been so intent on what the stranger had been saying and on Father Dennis's outbursts that I had not noticed others' reactions. Now I realized that several were muttering in support of Father Dennis. Someone—it sounded like Grandfather Tony's anxious voice—said something about not being as daft as Philip, and another asked how we would eat the money, and another growled about the black stone bringing the Upheaval.

With such support Father Dennis burst out, "There's

a dozen of us to the five of you! If you want your coal, try and get it!' "

Again for a long moment, the stranger Rhys looked down at Father Dennis's angry face. "We don't seem to be understanding one another," he said, and again he spoke to the Headman. "We don't intend you any harm; we do not want your land. We want just to come through and look over there"—he nodded towards the Forbidden Area—"to see if, by chance, there is good coal there. We have heard, from some of our old people, about a very good mine somewhere here, a mine that was—"

But at the word "mine," Father Dennis could no longer keep a hold on his anger. "What do you mean?" he shouted. "It's not yours, it's ours!"

A smile, mingled with puzzlement, lit the stranger's face; and one of the other strangers, overhearing, called, "They'll never understand, Rhys!"

Again, and patiently, the man Rhys tried to explain. "I was talking about a coal mine. A coal mine is where coal was dug out of the ground. It's a deep hole in the ground with . . ." he hesitated for a moment as Father Dennis, recognizing the reference to the Forbidden Area, growled afresh. "We will pay for the coal, of course," the stranger went on. "If the coal is there we will pay for it, and with the money you will be able to buy whatever you want."

"We've got all we want!" This time it was Grandfather Tony's quavering voice that interrupted him. "We can grow our food and keep our stock and—and—" The old man, perhaps astonished at his own daring, wavered into silence.

The stranger smiled, not unkindly, at him. "You think you have all that you need?" he asked.

"Of course we have!" began Father Dennis, but another outburst from him was cut short by a sudden question.

"What are you thinking we need?"

It was Father Alan who had spoken and, as ever, in his gentle voice. Father Dennis turned angrily on him, shouting that he would betray us all as his father, Philip, would have done. "You'll bring back the Upheaval, you with your ideas of—of progress!" He spat out the word, in his anger Father Dennis was confusing Father Alan with Grandfather Philip and what had been called his madness.

Father Alan appeared unmoved by Father Dennis's outburst. He seemed scarcely to have heard it. He remained looking up at the stranger, still waiting for an answer.

Before he spoke, the man Rhys looked across at the tangle of brambles and growth and hummocks of earth that made the Waste. "As a beginning," he said to Father Alan, "you could clear some of this ground. That would give you more land to live on; it could perhaps in time provide you with food to sell. And with the money from that you could . . ." He paused a moment, his dark eyes catching the hunting clubs and sickles and tools that we were holding and then, farther back, looking along the Mothers and the Grandmothers in their heavy woollen tunics and trews. "You could buy better tools and—and other things," he went on. "You could buy better equipment for your houses, for instance, and the more of this waste ground you cleared the more—"

Again Father Dennis could not hold back the thoughts that were swelling his anger. "Clear the Waste!" he cried. "Look at it, you fool! How would you fell all the trees, dig out the roots, get it level enough—"

The stranger Rhys did not, that time, wait for Father Dennis's anger to exhaust itself. He cut in, his voice not sharp but suddenly penetrating, "With machines, of course!"

"Machines?" echoed three or four voices, and I caught Susan's among them.

"Yes—machines!" the stranger went on. "Machines driven by coal that will drag away these tangles, that will pull down the trees, that will pull a heavy harrow to level the earth, and a plow so that—"

"Show them, Rhys!" It was another of the strangers who had called out. "Let them see for themselves!"

"It's the only way!" called another.

The man Rhys hesitated for a moment. "All right," he called back, and one of the strangers gave a shrill whistle. For a moment nothing happened. To us, Rhys began, "You'd better keep back out of the way—"

A sudden burst of clanking and hissing, the noises we had heard before but now much nearer, broke out. It seemed to come from lower down the trackway and was accompanied by tearing and crashing sounds as if some great object was forcing its way through the trees. And it was coming nearer and nearer. We saw smoke puffing up and then, round a bend in the trackway, there lumbered into sight—

"It's a carz!"

I caught Susan's excited cry before others were taking up the word, echoing it with mingled fear and wonderment and disbelief and consternation.

There could be no doubt about it. Though it was bigger than the one Susan and I had seen, it was unquestionably moving itself. In front was a kind of small platform on which stood a man apparently working a handle before him; the rear part was boxlike and big enough for six or eight people to stand in. And close behind the man rose a kind of long metal tube out of which smoke puffed while steam hissed out underneath. Using only its own strength it came on up the trackway, the spikes on its iron wheels gripping the ground. Even as we watched, some in amazement, more fearful, it demonstrated at least one of its skills by thrusting aside a small tree that had sprung up in its path and would have taken hours of digging to remove. But such a slight ability we scarcely noticed. With mingled horror and fascination we stared at it as, with a kind of inner determination, it lumbered ever nearer. Some of us had turned away as if to run but had been stayed by the unbelievable strangeness of the thing, and so intent were we all that few of us noticed the other strangers steady their horses against their unease at the rising noise, and guide them aside from the machine's path. Nor, as the clamor and the puffing grew ever louder, did we heed the man Rhys's warning shout—

though whether it was intended for us or for the worker of the machine no one could afterwards decide. Then we only stared at it thrusting its way forward towards the tree trunk that blocked the track.

And nearest that tough obstacle stood Father Dennis, angry disbelief in every line of his heavy body. He was gripping his hunting club and shouting as if to defy the machine to crash through the tree trunk.

The stranger who was guiding it could have had no intention of trying the machine against such an obstacle. And above the din he could not have heard the man Rhys's call. The guiding man must have thought that Rhys's intention was to demonstrate the feebleness, the futility, of our defenses, for he steered the machine aside from the tree trunk in order, it looked, to make a way through our thorny barricade. But in doing so, the machine lurched on the uneven ground tilting towards the brook, and at that moment, with a shout that we caught even above the machine's clamor, Father Dennis jerked himself forward to stop the attack.

The next few moments are tangled in all our memories. One moment the machine was lurching on the sloping ground, then with a twist of his handle the steering man righted it so that its spiked wheels gripped the earth. At once it was crashing on again through the thorn fence as Father Dennis, club upraised, hurled his great bulk towards it. And then came his angry, bewildered, agonized cry as one of the machine's heavy wheels flung him down and crushed him.

I have only a confused recollection of what followed.

I remember an interval of stunned silence shattered by Carole's scream, and a sudden, gasping cry, and then an anguished wail from Grandmother Mary. I remember seeing Stephen blunder forward though the machine had jerked to a stop almost as it struck and we could all see that he could not help Father Dennis. Then came an outburst of cries that increased in fear, and a sudden crashing through the undergrowth as some of us fled from the horror. I recall Grandfather Tony's face blank with utter disbelief.

More than the suddenness and the stark fact that Father Dennis had been killed had struck us all. In our tight little community all were familiar with death from sickness, from accident, from old age, but here was death brought crudely and violently by a monstrous machine— one of the very causes of the Upheaval from which long ago the Founder had led us to safety. There can have been scarcely one among us who did not feel impelled to run away, or to shout—as Grandfather Brian did—that the strangers could take their black, evil coal if only they would go and leave us in peace.

Nor can I tell how it was that some of us stayed. Probably the shock held us. We just stood staring with numbed horror at Father Dennis as the cries of those fleeing back to the village faded and the stillness of the Waste returned.

Not until then did we notice that the stranger Rhys first, and then the others, had got down from their horses and without looking our way had gone over to where Father Dennis lay. They scarcely needed to look at him before Rhys took off his fine-clothed tunic and laid it over the dead man's face.

Then Rhys whispered a word to the others and alone walked slowly towards us through the gap that Father Dennis had with such futility tried to defend. He spoke to Grandfather Peter. "He was a brave man," he said with difficulty, "but he didn't understand. And we didn't understand either."

The Headman lifted his eyes to look at him, and under the weatherworn color of his skin his face had gone suddenly grey and he looked an old man. Without a word he turned away and began to stumble back through the Waste.

A look of hopelessness passed over the stranger's face. He turned almost desperately to Father Alan. "I—I know you will find it hard to believe," he began, "but we had no idea—we'd never seen before . . ."

"You hadn't?" asked Father Alan. "Then you didn't know?"

For a long moment the stranger Rhys and Father Alan looked at each other, and there was the same horror on both their faces. It matched what we were all feeling. For the strangers as much as for us, it was the first time there had been such a death, the first time that their machine had done so terrible an act.

At last Rhys asked slowly, as if choosing his words, "If it would be any help—and if we wouldn't be intruding at such a time—we know how you all must be feeling . . ." He hesitated as if watching Father Alan's face for any sign of anger or outrage. "We have our horses," he went on. "It would be an easier way to carry him to—to wherever you want him taken . . . that is, if your people would not feel we were intruding."

Father Alan hesitated and then, as if realizing that with the Headman gone and Father Dennis dead, there was no one who could make a decision, he said quietly, "It would be a help."

We waited while the strangers lifted Father Dennis on to the back of one of their horses and then, still dismounted, turned towards us as if expecting to be guided to our village. Father Alan and Father Timothy led the way with Rhys walking between them. The rest of us followed—and I saw that John had stayed, too, and Mother Rachel and Mother Mavis. Beside us as we walked came the dismounted strangers. I found myself walking between Susan and a little, wizened stranger who gave me a quick, sad smile.

As we left we heard the machine start up afresh and several of us looked back in alarm. But it was going backwards, away from our pathetic defense. The little old stranger walking beside me said, "Don't worry, lad. We'll not bring it again, not unless your people should come to want it."

We followed the track that led past the Forbidden Area, the track down which, I guessed, the coal had long ago been carried in machines. I knew that the telltale blackness was all about the place; I knew that the stranger walking slowly beside me must see it.

Susan must have realized that too, for she flashed a glance at me. The stranger's old eyes were quick enough to catch her glance, and to interpret it.

"Don't you worry about that, girl," he said, "I reckon after today's happenings we'll seek elsewhere. I reckon Rhys has decided that too high a price has already been paid for any coal that may be there. We'll not trouble you again."

The New Beginning

LOOKING BACK NOW, it seems almost strange how the next morning we went about our work as ever. It had to be done, we all knew, for the land and the seasons wait on no one's feelings. The only difference I can remember was that it was Father Alan who told us what work to do and not, as had been usual, one of the Grandfathers. And that we seemed to have little to say to one another.

The next day passed and the next in the usual work, though at some time Father Alan must have arranged with Grandfather Tony to make a long box for Father Dennis's body; and the next day, since the Forbidden Area had become meaningless, he was buried where the lower pasture ended at the Waste.

Afterwards we waited near the door to the Grand-parents' House. We expected that the Headman would address us, as he had done about Old Carz, but it seemed Grandfather Peter was not in his room.

For a while we stood about aimlessly. It was too near dusk to think of starting new work—though Grand-mother Ruth and Mother Janet had, of course, gone to the milking—and it was too soon to be going to our Houses to end the day.

It was then that Father Alan called to us to gather not in the Grandparents' House but in the Children's. He must, I think, have had a word with some of the Grand-parents and Parents for no one questioned that he, not yet a Grandfather and unskilled in the Reading and Writ-ing, should have seemed to take the leading of us. Most of us followed into the House, and without any bidding arranged ourselves as well as we could. We children sat on the floor, the Mothers and Fathers and those of the Grandparents who came sat on our little stools—I remem-ber Grandmother Mary nearly toppling off hers—or squatted on our bunks.

Father Alan said, "There are things we must decide. It seems Peter has taken himself up to the hut—at least for a time." We all knew that he was referring to Old Carz' hut; we left unspoken our guesses as to why the Headman should have gone there.

Father Alan went on in his quiet, steady voice. He told us that, on the day of the invasion, the stranger Rhys had repeated his offer to clear the Waste for us. "He told me as we brought Dennis back," said Father Alan. "He told me they would do it whether there was any coal to be found or not."

"But they'll still be after the coal," said Grandfather Brian, disbelieving.

"And they'll bring their devilish machine," quavered Grandfather Tony. "They'll crush and—and destroy and—"

"That was an accident," said Father Alan steadily. "They knew no more than we what Dennis would do." He waited a moment before he went on. "The strangers have made us the offer to clear the Waste at least as far as the new fence. They will do it without any pay—"

"They'll still be wanting the coal!" burst out Stephen, surprising us all that he should have been so moved as to join in adults' talk.

Father Alan answered him as if Stephen had been a Parent. "The man Rhys has given me his word," he said. "If we will allow him to look for the coal, he will pay for what he finds. If we would prefer him not to look for it, he will still clear as much of the Waste to the fence as he can."

A buzz of puzzlement spread through the House.

"Clear the Waste—for nothing?" asked Grandfather Brian as if not understanding.

"It would make a fine pasture," said Father Timothy.

"But they'll have to bring their carz!" blurted out Stephen.

"And how will they pay us?" Grandfather Tony asked

querulously. "What use will their metal, their money, be to us?"

For a moment Father Alan did not answer. Then he said, "There are many things we have not understood. We have heard that the old ways of living brought the Upheaval. We have never heard how the people lived before the Upheaval."

"That's like Old Carz' tales!" exclaimed Stephen almost angrily.

But there were some who looked sharply at him—though whether because as Grandparents and Parents they thought he should not so speak in their presence, or whether because they had, like Father Alan, come to realize the truth in the old man's stories, I cannot say. I remember Mother Mavis saying, "Old Carz was right about his carz! We all know that now!" And though there was bitterness in her voice, there was also undeniable belief. And recalling that Mother Mavis had unwittingly echoed Susan's words, I looked for Susan and saw that hint of a smile I had come to know.

Father Alan waited until the voices had quieted. Then he went on. "I think if we all listen for a little while we may understand more about the old days. They had many ideas that could help us, ideas the strangers have come to understand and to use. Such ideas could help us to get better tools, and finer cloth like the strangers wear; and horses and—"

"And a carz!" blurted Stephen angrily.

For once, for the only time I can recall, Father Alan

raised his voice. "Yes!" he replied almost defiantly. "And a carz if we should come to want one! It could help us with the plowing and the harrowing. It would help us grow more food—"

"For money?" called Grandfather Brian, distrusting.

"What good would that do?" quavered Grandfather Tony.

Father Alan was never one to say much and for a moment he seemed to have to gather his thoughts afresh. When he spoke again, it was in his usual quiet tone. "Old Carz has left a writing about it and Gerald here has puzzled some of it out and—"

Again a babble of voices rose up, but this time there was more puzzlement than anger, more surprise than fear.

"What does it say, Gerald?" Mother Rachel called, and Grandfather Tony quavered more in surprise than alarm, "Can you read Old Carz' writing?" Father Timothy, too, asked to know what the old man had said.

"It's hard," Father Alan said for me. "But if you'll listen . . ." And he looked at me questioningly.

I had never for a moment seen myself doing such a thing. My fingers trembled as I pulled out Old Carz' crumpled writings from under my tunic; and for what seemed a long time I stared at my own clumsy letters, hardly able to recall what they said. I began, I remember, with the first page, with the old man's account of his childhood, but almost at once Father Alan said gently, "Leave that for now, lad. Go on to where he tells about making and selling."

I think now that, as Father Alan and the stranger Rhys had walked back to the village after the invasion, Rhys must have explained something of what Old Carz had been trying to tell me. For as I began to read, stumbling among the phrases I could recognize, Father Alan now and again prompted me. Together we went on, I reading a phrase or two, Father Alan adding a few words in explanation, and so telling something of how, in the old days, some people had made all kinds of strange things and other people had grown the food for all; and that by means of money, each side had been able to buy what they needed—

"It's like a shopz!" Grandmother Mary called out. "It's like he used to say—a shopz!" And her round face stared at us in amazement at her own understanding.

And in the excited babble that followed, Father Alan and I seemed not to have to explain any more—at least not at that time. Many questions were to come later, and many uncertainties, too; but that afternoon we had come to understand enough for the moment, for the decision.

As the voices at last quieted, Father Alan repeated the pale strangers' offer. "The man Rhys has told me where I can find him," he added. "It's near a day's walk away. Do you want me to go and tell him that we accept his offer: to clear the Waste for us and then, if we allow him to find the coal, to accept his money for it?"

A half-dozen voices agreed to his going. But suddenly Grandfather Tony struggled to his feet. "But what if it brings back the Upheaval, too?" he tried to shout. "What if these machines and—and shopz and wonders bring back the fighting and destroying and the—the—"

It was Stephen who took up the old man's point. "What has Old Carz got to tell us about that?" he demanded, glaring at me.

It was, I realized with a sudden sickening, in the part of Old Carz' writings that I had not yet read, the part he had begun to write and then, in order that I might get a clearer picture of the Old Days, had left unfinished on what I had at first mistaken for his last sheet. Even before I looked down at the sheet. I had caught the look of triumph in Stephen's eyes. I saw that in my hurry to read as much of the old man's story as I could, I had not even filled in many of the letters of those first-written lines. Only two or three phrases were readable and they, out of their contexts, told nothing . . . until my bewildered eyes put a few words together, and I remembered the time when Old Carz had himself begun to read them aloud. I remembered sufficient to begin, haltingly, about the time that would come when we found out about machines and bombs and suchlike again, and we must not allow them "to shape our lives so that we came to destroy what we have created. . . ."

I had managed to read enough, just enough, for Father Alan to be able to guess at what Old Carz must have intended. With a smile at me, he said, "Gerald is still very new to the Reading. But what Old Carz meant is clear enough. As we have seen, these machines—and the other things, too—can destroy, but, as in the Old Days they helped, too, so they can help us. We must make sure to use them to help—"

"How can we?" Stephen demanded, and Grandfather Tony quavered, "If we let them come back, there's no telling . . ."

It was Grandmother Mary who unexepectedly answered them. "Because we know," she said in a suddenly determined tone. "Because we've seen what a carz can do, we know it—its dangers. And so with the other things —we know they brought the Upheaval and—and—"

Mother Rachel added, quickly, "We must pass on what we know. We must tell our grandchildren of the wonders so that they can rediscover more of them, but we must tell them, too, of the dangers . . ."

"When they've learned the skills that we have lost," added Father Alan, "they will know the dangers, too."

Stephen's face still looked heavily sullen. "What good will that do now?" he asked.

No one answered him. No doubt many of us were still uncertain, but we had come to realize that we had to go on, we had to accept that we could no longer live in seclusion.

Father Alan turned again to the stranger Rhys's offer and asked if he should accept it. Only two or three sat silent. The rest of us nodded or called our agreement.

So it was that the next morning through the early light Father Alan and Father Harold set out. Though ever and again as we worked we looked towards the Waste, towards the Forbidden Area that was no longer forbidden, hoping to see them returning, we did not expect them before the next day. But to our surprise they came back that same evening, and riding on horses, and with them came the man Rhys and the little old stranger who had spoken to Susan and me and whom we now learned was called Dai. We all gathered at the yard-gate to welcome them, of course, and yet on both sides we had little to say.

The two strangers lodged that night in the Grandparents' House and there must have been much talk by rushlight before they all went to sleep. It was quiet talk for we children, though we lay long awake at the strangeness of it all, never once heard a voice raised in anger or alarm. And by next morning when the two strangers came to go, it seemed that agreement had been reached: in a few days they would come back with their machine to begin clearing the Waste and later, when that had been done, they would seek for their coal and pay us according to what they found.

We all gathered at the yard-gate to see them go, and it was then that Rhys, in his gentle, singsong voice, said, "If you would allow us, we would like to give you a few presents." His quick eyes flashed along our faces to make sure that none was offended before he pulled open a sack that hung by his saddle. In it were things like the pedlars had brought on their very rare visits to our valley, things we had never thought to possess: bright cloths for the Mothers and Grandmothers, fine knives and strange clipping tools for the men, and sticks of colored stuff that made marks on the sheets of paper he gave us children. And I noticed that the little old one, Dai, suddenly caught up a narrow length of blue cloth, shinier than I had ever seen, and with a smile threw it to Susan.

"What is it?" she asked, delighted but puzzled at its narrowness.

"A ribbon, girl, to tie back your hair," said the old stranger. "And it's just the color for you!"

The strangers kept their word. Within the week we heard their machine chuffing up towards the Forbidden Area, and soon there began the crashing of trees as its great strength tore them down. But though some of us, when we could, went down to peer through the trees at what they were doing, the strangers rarely came to the village. Instead, they had built huts in the Waste and kept themselves to themselves, though now and again if one or another saw us watching he waved.

It was a long job, and at times there must have been about a dozen men at work there. And we found that their machine had a trick we could never have guessed. A kind of saw, not straight like ours but a huge round one, could be attached to it and then the machine's strength used to saw the felled trees at a speed which made us gasp in astonishment. I remember Grandfather Tony standing by me as we watched, exclaiming, "What couldn't I do with a saw like that!"

Long before the Waste had been cleared, several great piles of wood had been stacked along near the lower pasture. We assumed that the strangers would carry them away, but one day Rhys came up to the village to ask where we would like the wood stored. "It'll keep you going a while when it's seasoned," he said, and then, catching Father Alan's surprise, he added, "We agreed that the Waste is yours. The timber's part of it."

Several times during the next few days their great machine rumbled up to our village dragging a cart with a load of sawn wood. Susan and John and I helped the Fathers to unload it and stack it in the yard, and more round behind the barn. Never before had we been so rich in wood.

On one such visit of the machine Susan ventured to ask the round-faced stranger who worked it how the coal drove it. He told us that the coal boiled the water in a great container the machine carried; and that the steam, as it tried to escape, was forced along pipes in order to push at what he called pistons which, as they were so urged into movement, turned the wheels. Though we had noticed the steam puffing and hissing as it strove to get away, we were amazed that it had the strength to move the whole machine.

"Did all the carz work like that?" Susan asked.

The stranger smiled. "It's not truly a car," he said. "They were smaller, and people rode in them." It seemed that such machines had differed from his for he spoke of their using "petrol" instead of coal; and he added that the "petrol" had been among the first things that the people had run short of, and that had "helped to start off the troubles." I guessed that by "the troubles" he meant what we called the Upheaval, and that shortage of the "petrol" had made it more difficult for workers in towns to get their food from faraway.

Another time when the man came with his machine, I asked him about the thin paper I had found, for I was still baffled by the word CRISPS after Smith's name. The man looked at it, frowning a little. "We've found such pieces," he said. "We found a whole lot of them in a place that had once been a shop. As far as we could tell crisps were some kind of food."

"But why is Smith on it?" I asked.

"Perhaps a smith had used his fire for the cooking," he suggested; he spoke as if anyone who worked in metals was called Smith. The paper which had appeared to me significant was perhaps no more than a meaningless left-over from the Old Days.

Between such journeys, the machine went back to its work of dragging out tree roots and tearing up thickets of thorn and bramble, and levelling the Waste. And as the work went on, the spring days lengthened into summer and the oats began to ripen and the blackberries to cluster. And all that while Grandfather Peter stayed in the hut up by the Wall. We had not forgotten him, of course; indeed Father Alan and Grandmother Mary—and others, too, it was said—went up to ask him to come down, to live again in his room in the Grandparents' House. But always they came back to tell that he said he preferred to stay up there. So Carole, and sometimes Stephen with her, took to going up with his sack of stores—until, near on Harvest time, Carole was old enough to go into the Parents' House and, as we had long expected, she asked for Stephen to go with her.

That left me as oldest boy and Susan as oldest girl in the Children's House; and so we came to take Grandfather Peter's stores up to him.

I remember the first time we went. As we drew near to the hut, I felt a sense of pride stealing over me. Down the valley the strangers' machine was clanking at its work and so much of the Waste had been cleared that we were coming to speak of it as the New Pasture. And through what had once been so thick a growth that we had no notion of what lay beyond it, there spread out more fields, the fields of other strangers' villages that would, one day, link up with ours. And farther off we could just make out the distant cluster of buildings that we knew to be where Rhys and the others lived. The sight gave me a feeling of growing freedom, of escape from the narrow way of living that Grandfather Peter, and Grandfather Robert before him, had imposed on us.

I remember that, just as we reached the hut door, Susan looked at me, and I was surprised not to see a matching pride on her face. Indeed, she looked a little puzzled and a little disappointed, too.

Then Grandfather Peter opened the door. "Hallo," he said in so welcoming a voice that I hardly recognized it. "I'm glad you've come. I was getting a bit low on the oatmeal."

I must have stared at him as he took the sack from my hand and tipped its contents on the little table, the table on which Old Carz had made his writings. "What's this?" Grandfather Peter exclaimed. "Some mutton! It's good of Ruth to have spared that. And this?" he asked, holding up a piece of breadlike substance dotted with fruit.

"It's a new kind of bread," Susan told him. "The strangers call it 'cake.' One of them gave us the fruits. Grandmother Mary thought you might like a piece."

"I'm sure I shall," said the old man, and somehow he did not look as old as when I had last seen him.

He looked over our heads towards where the Waste had been. "Are you in a hurry?" he asked. "I've been trying to see what's been going on. They've made a fine job of it . . . but that pale grey line, there in the distance?" He pointed a long finger far beyond the land that sloped down from the Waste. "Is that the sea, do you know? I once saw what looked like a strange machine moving across it."

Susan stared at the sight in wonder, but the old man's appearance still held me. He looked more at ease than I had ever known him.

He caught my staring eyes and just for a moment I saw the old look come into his face, the watchful hardness in his eyes though his lips still smiled. I waited for him to speak—though I did not know what I expected him to say.

At last he went on. "As you see, I've been up to the spring for my water. Yes, I can still get about quite a bit.

And tell your fa—tell Father Alan that, when the oats are ready to cut, I'll give a hand as usual. I like cutting the oats; there's a soothing, purposeful feel about it."

Susan and I left him soon after that. I remember that he watched us from the hut door as we scrambled over the boulders that had once been the middle of the dam; and I remember, too, that as we reached the smoother path Susan glanced at me with a questioning look in her eyes.

"You didn't find much to say to him," she commented.

"I—but he wasn't like I'd expected! He . . . well, if he had understood all along? . . . And the way he used to act, as if he didn't know about carz and such, as if he thought Old Carz was a fool, when all the time . . ."

"He's still acting now, isn't he?" Susan asked. "He's acting as if he believes that what we're doing is all right, as if he believes that it'll not lead again to the Upheaval."

"But why? . . ." I began.

She looked at me not sideways but directly. "It's what we're all doing, isn't it? We're all pretending that the Upheaval can't come again. We're all acting as if we're sure."

We thought that after Harvest—and Grandfather Peter did join in—the strangers would leave the Waste for a while. To be sure, the New Pasture was still rough in places and would need more levelling and plowing before it could be sown with grass. But to our surprise, the strangers stayed on in their huts and soon we heard other new sounds coming from what had been the Forbidden Area. When we had time we went down to peer at what they were doing, and saw that they had used some of the bigger balks of timber to erect the skeleton of a building, like those we had seen in rusted iron, over the hole in the Forbidden Area. And they had brought long, thick rope with them, far longer and thicker than any we had known and, by hanging it over a great wheel, were contriving to go down that black-rimmed hole in search of the coal.

Watching them, I suddenly realized what they would soon be finding. I turned away with the idea of hurrying back to find Father Alan and tell him—for the secrecy that had once been impressed upon me seemed no longer to hold in the changes that had so rapidly come to us. But as I turned, the old stranger Dai called to me to wait; it seemed that he, too, wanted to speak with Father Alan.

"I've heard tell that you know the trick of writing," the old man said to me. "So you'll be needed."

I must have looked surprised for I had assumed that the strangers knew all about the Reading and Writing.

His wizened face wrinkled more deeply in a smile. "Most of us know how to write," he said, "but I was reckoned rather old to start learning. And there are some names we'll need to know and only you'll be able to write them for me."

I guessed what names he was thinking of; I guessed that already some of the strangers had used their great rope to lower themselves down into the hole in search of the coal. And I knew what they must have found there.

When we talked with Father Alan, I realized that he, too, knew.

"Do the best you can for them," he told old Dai. "And these boxes you're going to make for them, we'll bury them at the edge of the New Pasture." As old Dai looked at him in question, he added, "We laid Dennis there."

The old stranger nodded. "And this lad of yours," he asked, "he can write the names for me, can he? We have the custom of putting up boards so that any passersby will know, and I've the job of making the boards and I want to get the letters right. Have you something to write with?"

I had. I had the colored sticks that the stranger Rhys had given us tucked away in safety under my bunk, and I ran to fetch them. Old Dai had thought to bring a sheet of paper.

As Father Alan said the names, I wrote them as well as I could. There were more than I had known, and some must have been children who had never grown to become parents. And there was Grandfather Philip's name among them; and . . .

Father Alan hesitated before he told me to write "both names." So I wrote down: "OLD CARZ OR GREAT-GRAND-FATHER PAUL."

Old Dai had listened, but when Father Alan gave him the list, he asked: "And the other one—Dennis, I think you called him—surely he's to have his name-board, too?"

"Of course," said Father Alan, and my surprise at the suggestion ebbed away.

At last the old stranger had the list complete. "I'll get all arranged as soon as I can," he told Father Alan. "If this lad of yours will just show me the place? . . ."

I walked beside him back to the fringe of what had been the Waste, to where a little patch of uneven grass still showed where we had laid Father Dennis. Old Dai looked at it, but curiously he seemed more interested not in the actual patch of ground but that it was, as he said, "just about the middle of the valley." He added, as if in explanation, "Perhaps that's as it should be."

I must still have looked puzzled. We had, I knew, chosen the place because it was between the Waste and what had been the lower pasture, and it was above the brook's flooding.

Old Dai smiled. "You've never heard tell of the old days?" he asked.

"The time of the Upheaval?" I asked. "I know about—"

He was shaking his grizzled head. "Long before then," he said. "Very long before then." He waved an arm over beyond the Mountain. "Over that way was Wales," he said. "And over the other way was England. And in the old days, long before what you call the Upheaval, the men from Wales and the men from England used to fight over this land. Have you never heard tell of that?"

"No," I said.

He glanced down at the little patch of still-uneven ground. "It seems right in a way that it should be here," he said. "It seems right that the poor fellow, and a brave one, too, should lie where we've come to meet and to become friends, I hope."

The strangers did not, as we expected, stop working as the winter set in. Only when the snow came—and that winter it lay for only a few days—did the sounds of their working cease. Often, as we worked outdoors or as we stood awhile at the yard-gate looking with pride towards what we were forgetting to call the Forbidden Area, we heard the sounds of movements and, often, the clamor of their machine as it rumbled away down the valley below the New Pasture. Their machine was, we heard, dragging carts after it, carts laden with coal—but we also heard that the mine, as the strangers called it, was not the rich one they had been seeking; it had, the man Rhys explained to Father Alan, "only enough to keep us going for a while."

We heard this when, early in March, Rhys came bringing a small sack with him. We children—and probably the Parents and the Grandparents, too—guessed that he had brought some new wonders to show us, to give us perhaps in payment. And so he had, but not quite as we expected.

We gathered in the Grandparents' House, sitting on their beds or squatting on the floor, while Rhys asked us to clear a space in the middle. Then, taking his little sack, he turned it upside-down and out fell—

There were hundreds and hundreds of them, little round pieces of metal, some brown-colored, some silver.

For a moment we gaped in astonishment, and then, as someone gasped that it was money, we all began grabbing pieces, looking at them, turning them over. I snatched two brown ones of different sizes. They showed, I quickly saw, some strange writing much worn, and in the center what looked like the impress of a woman's head and shoulders, a Mother I guessed her to be, with on her head a curious, spiky kind of hat.

In our excitement and wonder at the strangeness of the money, and at the hundreds and hundreds of them that Rhys had brought with him, it took several warnings to us not to lose any of them, and some of the Fathers and Grandparents began to collect them into a pile. But we had so many questions to ask and so many possibilities to voice.

"It'll buy yards and yards of that fine cloth!"

"And lots of—of ribbon!" I heard Susan recall the word.

"And colored sticks to write with!" I shouted.

"And a new plow!"

"And that spade that's broken—"

"And two buckets are past mending. We'll be able to get—"

Curiously it was, again, Grandfather Tony's quavering voice that somehow pierced our excitement. "Would it," he called to the stranger Rhys, "would it get us a new bull? Old Brown Tom, he's been good, but by next autumn we'll have to be thinking . . ."

The smile on Rhys's face must have checked Grandfather Tony rather than the old man's uncertainty. We all waited for the stranger's answer.

He spoke, as ever, in his gentle singsong. "Yes, it will buy you a new bull. It will buy you a new cow or two as well, and perhaps some of the new tools you've been needing. And"—he flashed a quick smile towards Mother Rachel—"you may even have enough left over for a few lengths of new cloth, too. And"—he raised his voice just a little so that for a few moments longer we held back our returning excitement—"and this is our first payment. We shall be able to bring you more."

"More!" exclaimed Grandfather Brian in disbelief.

"Yes," replied Rhys. "Every few months, for two or three years at least, we shall be able to bring you more money. After that we cannot tell. There may be more coal left in your mine, or we may have to look elsewhere. But for two or three years at least—"

We could no longer hold in our excitement. We all of us had to voice our wonder, our amazement at the possibilities opening out before us.

"We could have a dozen cows!"

"And one of those round saws!" That was Grandfather Tony's voice.

"And fine cloth to wear—of an evening, of course!"

"And more colored sticks to write with!" I shouted.

"And we could get some pigs! Pig meat tastes better—"

"And new cooking pots, three or four of them!"

But, as he squatted watching us, the smile on the man Rhys's face faded a little, and one by one we quieted as we became aware that he had more to tell us. I remember catching a scowl on Stephen's face as if he suspected a snag, and the corners of Carole's mouth drooped a little, and the hint of a frown puckered Susan's forehead.

At last we were waiting for Rhys to go on. "You can have all those things and many more," he said slowly, "but it will take time. And the day will come when there will be no more coal in the mine, no more that we will be able to get out safely. So"—he flashed a glance at Father Alan —"you will have to plan carefully before you spend your money."

He waited a moment as if expecting someone to challenge him.

"I know only a little of the way you live here," he went on, "but we have down near our town other farmers. They have many of the things you would like to have, but first they built up their farms, spent their money on new and better stock, on new and better tools. In your New Pasture you could keep more cattle; perhaps in time you could keep more and better sheep on your hills, and perhaps keep pigs, too. And it is from those—from selling the meat and the wool and the hides that you will be able to get the money to buy what you will come to need, so that when there is no coal left in the mine . . ."

Some of us must have looked disappointed; we had thought to have at least a few of the new wonders almost at once. The man Rhys quickly saw the changes on our faces. "It will take time and work," he said. "It depends on how you spend your money and on how well you plan your work."

Soon after that, as I remember it, Rhys and Father Alan and Grandfather Brian went into the Headman's room, and there, I suppose, Rhys must have explained more, perhaps made other suggestions as to how our new money might best be spent.

We children went out into the yard and waited there, as did also Carole and Stephen though they were now reckoned among the Parents. I went with Susan and John to look over the yard-gate at the New Pasture and the land opening out below it while we waited to see the man Rhys leave. I remember overhearing Stephen tell Carole how many new cattle he reckoned the New Pasture might support. "That is," he added, "if we could clear even more of the Waste to grow the extra fodder they'll need. Or we could," he went on as a new thought struck him, "we might sell some of our extra cattle to the farmers lower down, for them to fatten for selling later. They'd give us money for them . . ."

Carole looked at him admiringly for having thought out such an idea, and Susan, catching Carole's look, smiled at me. I think that, at that moment, she was no more than amused at the sight of Carole and Stephen together as newcomers to the Parents' House; but I remember suddenly realizing that one day, in two or three years' time, Susan would be old enough to go into the Parents' House and that she might, as we were of an age, ask for me to go with her. And, strangely, I knew that I would be willing.

Rhys came out at last, mounted his horse, and we waved as he set off down the path that led now to the roadway beyond the mine. For a while we watched him go; then, as he disappeared through the belt of trees that marked where once the lower pasture had ended and the Forbidden Area had begun, we turned to go back into the Children's House.

Young John said, "He knows such a lot!" And then, with a glance toward the hut up the valley under the Wall, he asked, "Do you think Old Carz could have known it all?"

"Some of it," said Susan, "and in time we'll come to know more."

"What?" asked John. "All that people knew in the old days before the Upheaval?"

"I don't know about that," said Susan. "But we'll know something that they didn't know until too late."

John looked at her, puzzled for the moment, and then both he and I knew what she was thinking. But she didn't add any more. Instead, remembering that she was now oldest girl, she exclaimed, "Here am I chattering when there's still the meal to get. Come on, both of you, and help—unless you want to go hungry to your bunks!"

G. R. KESTEVEN writes he was "educated officially and not ineffectually at Hendon Grammar School and, as then family fortunes would not run to more, perhaps more effectively educated working at such diverse jobs as insurance, advertising, gardening, fire fighting and teaching." He started writing for the purpose of helping children with reading difficulties, and this lead to the publication of over thirty stories for children, under his real name of G. R. Crosher, many of which have been translated into foreign languages.

Most recently Mr. Kesteven has written historical nonfiction for use in schools, and a number of books on travel. He lives in Watford in Hertfordshire, England.